A Sign of
Sherlockian Realism:
Sherlock Holmes Cartoons
from a warped mind
Volume 2

By

Don Hobbs

Paperback ISBN 978-1-78705-861-3

Published by MX Publishing
335 Princess Park Manor, Royal Drive,
London, N11 3GX
www.mxpublishing.co.uk

Cover design by Brian Belanger

To

To John Bennett Shaw, who taught me how to collect and how to be a Sherlockian.

Contents

221 Sherlockian Aesthetic Realism drawings by Don Hobbs with a canonical explanation accompanying each.

Foreword

This all started in the fall of 2011 when my wife Joyce and I stumbled across the Napoleon Museum during our "Roaming Rome" vacation. Inside there was an art exhibit by Chiam Koppleman, the American artist known for his works of Aesthetic Realism. The exhibit was entitled 'Napoleon Enters New York' and it featured drawings and paintings of Napoleon in various unfamiliar settings, like entering Coney Island or riding alligators. His Bicones hat and his epaulette-coat were always present in the pictures and something about this exhibit struck a chord with me. Immediately I knew I had to start my own series of drawings. Thus was born Aesthetic Sherlockian Realism. The pipe and deerstalker replace the epaulettes and Bicones. The Master replaces the Emperor. So enjoy my artistic adventure where the game is afoot.

Sherlock Holmes in Paris

"It is likely that we should have gone to Paris tomorrow." NOBL

Sherlock Holmes
Bungie Jumping

"...Very good. Jump in, Watson..." CARD

Sherlock Holmes
In St. Louis, MO

"...and the other at St. Louis..." SIGN

Sherlock Holmes at the Empre State Building

"... the Randall Gang were arrested in New York this morning..." ABBE

Sherlock Holmes
Visits Disneyland

"...When his castle in the air fell down..." 3GAB

Sherlock Holmes at the Taj Mahal

"... and the story is still told in India..."   EMPT

Sherlock Holmes Rides a
Roller Coaster

"… up and down for some time, lost in thought…"   GOLD

Sherlock Holmes on a Deserted Island

"... of the singular adventures of the Grice Pattersons on the island of Uffa..."   FIVE

Sherlock Holmes
Sitting on a Wall

"…You then glanced up at the wall…" 3GAB

Sherlock Holmes
In Disguise

"...having removed his disguise, he sat before the fire and
laughed heartily in his silent..." CHAS

Sherlock Holmes Rides
A Segway

"... I saw the wheel tracks..."   GREE

Sherlock Holmes
On a Pogo—Stick

"...It's not a time to stick at trifles..." BRUC

Sherlock Holmes
Celebrates Thanksgiving

"...there was bright moonlight outside..." PRIO

Sherlock Holmes
In a Hot–Air Balloon

"...It wasn't hot air, either..." ILLU

Sherlock Holmes Ironing
His Clothes

"... we must strike when the iron is hot..." CARD

Sherlock Holmes
Disguised as a Snowman

"...His footmarks had pressed right through the snow..." ILLU

Sherlock Holmes
Rides a Unicycle

"...shot my syringe full of aniseed over the hind wheel..."
MISS

Sherlock Holmes in a Burka

"... you have been in Afghanistan, I perceive..."   STUD

Sherlock Holmes at The John Hancock Building

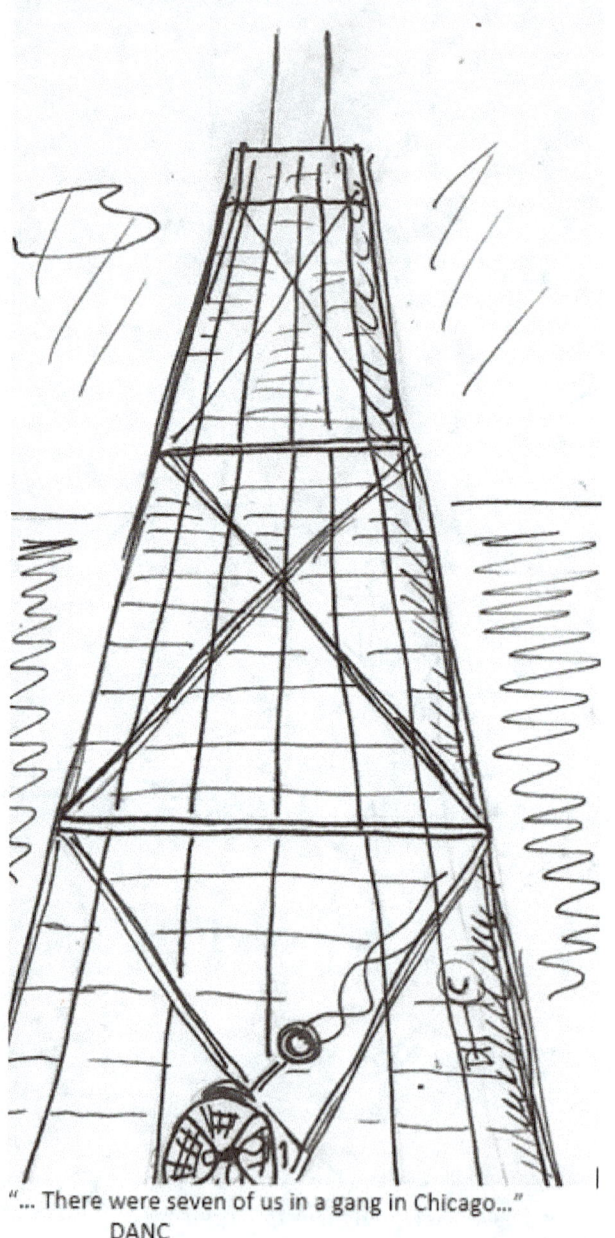

"... There were seven of us in a gang in Chicago..."
DANC

Sherlock Holmes Pole Vaults

"... into a hugh vault..." REDH

Sherlock Holmes Presents
Alfred Hitchcock

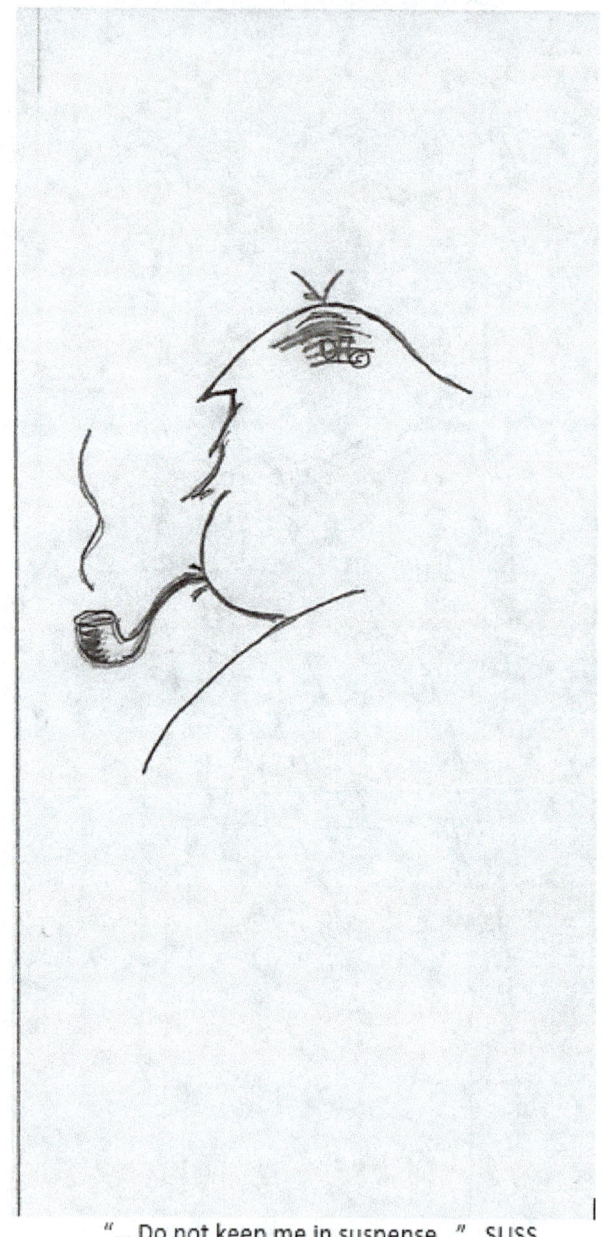

"... Do not keep me in suspense..." SUSS

Sherlock Holmes Visits
Reunion Tower

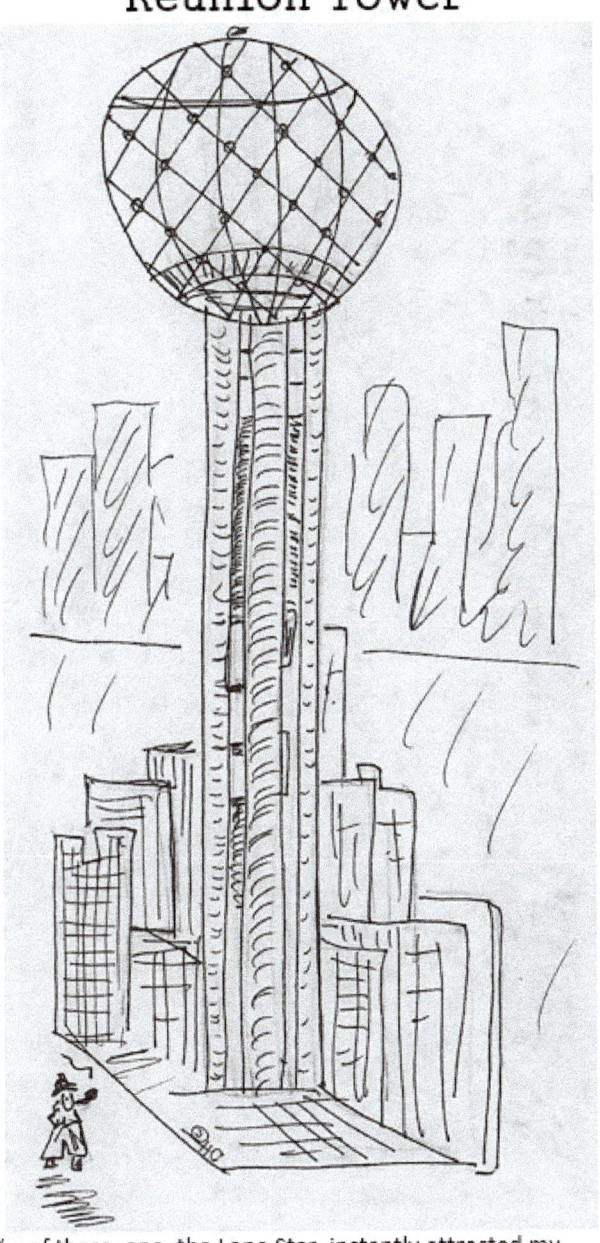

"... of these, one, the Lone Star, instantly attracted my attention..." FIVE

Sherlock Holmes in Front
Of a Tepee

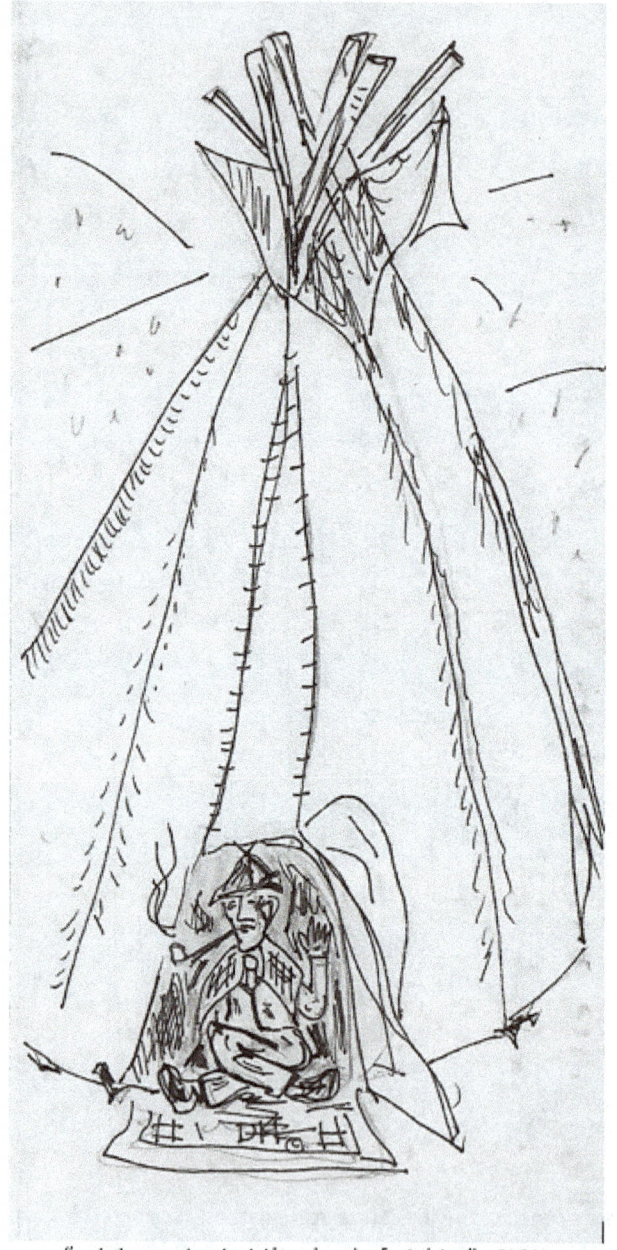

"... into my tent at the dead of night..."   SIGN

Sherlock Holmes Moth

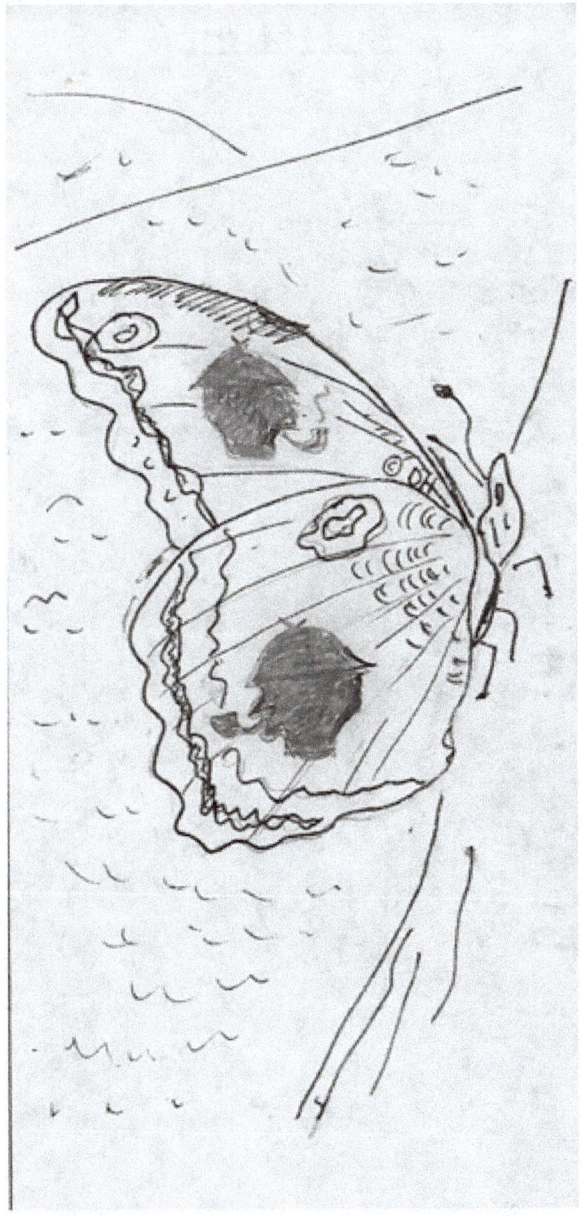

"...His grey clothes and jerky, zigzag, irregular progress made him not unlike some huge moth himself..." SIGN

Sherlock Holmes at a Bullfight

"... He bellowed like a bull and rushed for the door..."
GLOR

Sherlock Holmes in Kuala Lampur

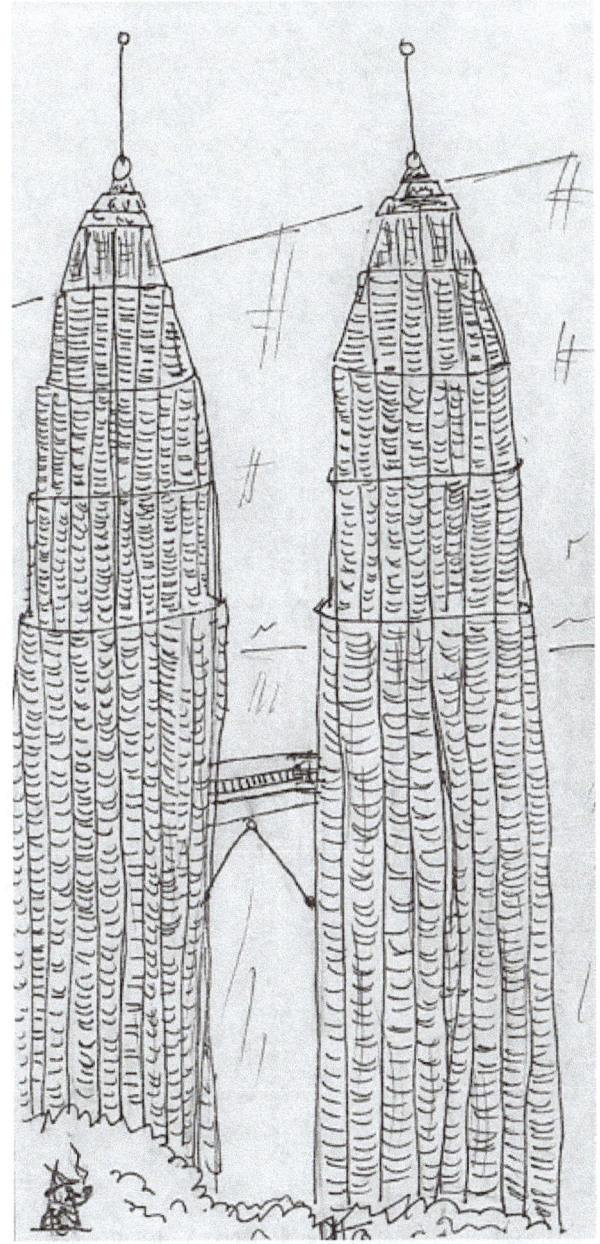

"… almost in the shadow of the great tower…" SECO

Sherlock Holmes Visits the Space Needle

"... near the borders of the Northwest Provinces..."
SIGN

Sherlock Holmes Mr. Potato Head

"... a cabbage and a potato..."   SIGN

Sherlock Holmes Visits
the Sergrada Familia

"… but I traced himback, Paris and Rome and Madrid
to Barcelona where his ship come in, in '86…"   WIST

Sherlock Holmes Goes Roller Blading

"...upon the long, smooth rollers..."   GLOR

Sherlock Holmes Visits Australia

"... Mr. Turner, who made money in Australia..." BOSC

Sherlock Holmes and an Obelisk

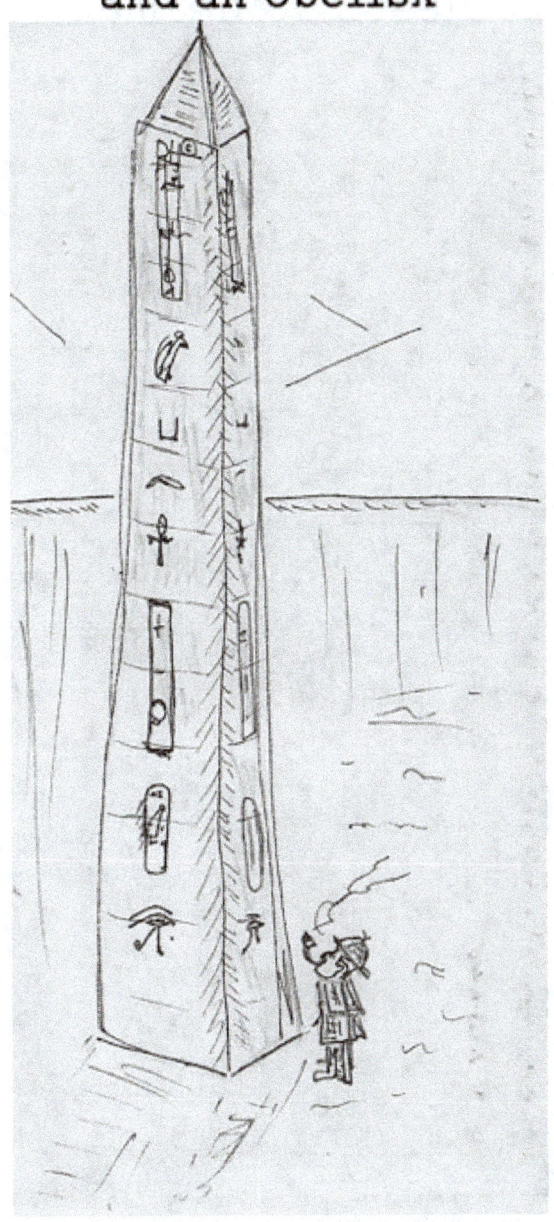

"...each side-pillar surmounted by mouldering heraldic emblems ..."   SOLI

Sherlock Holmes
Meets Spiderman

"... as the gentlest tremors of the edges of the web remind one of the foul spider whicjh lurks at the center..." NORW

Sherlock Holmes
Visits Planet X

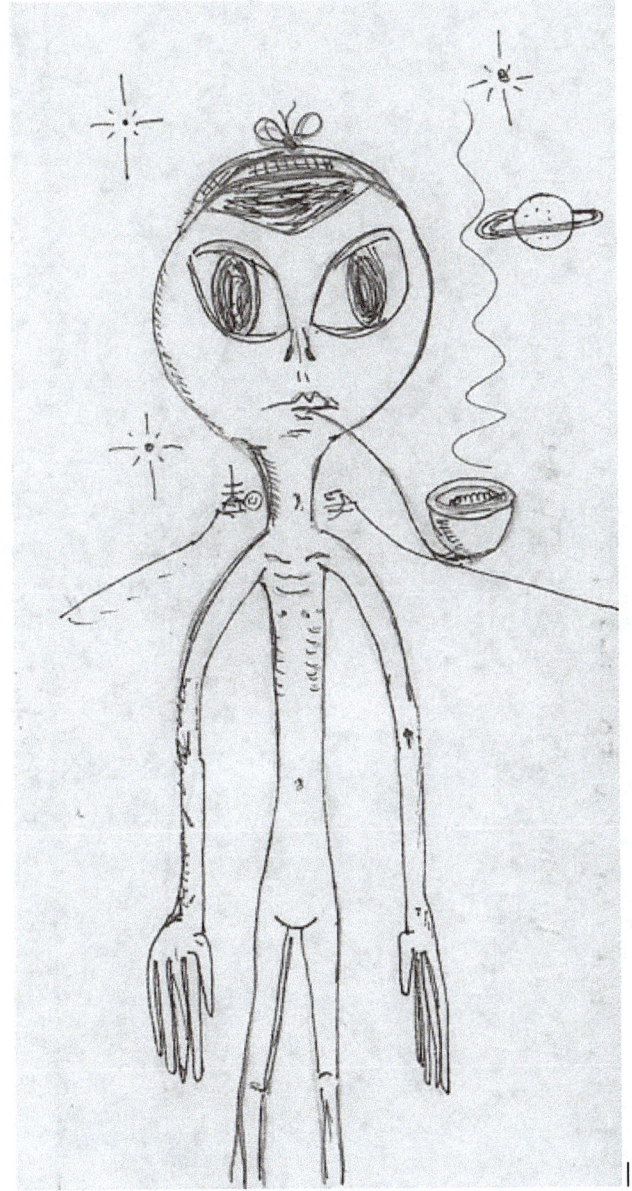

"... The lady began to show some curious traits quite alien
to her ordinary sweet and gentle disposition..." SUSS

Sherlock Holmes
Ski Jumping

"... The best men all left us, and the show began to go downhill..." VEIL

Sherlock Holmes Visits Haight—Ashbury

"... Slowly it rose from our souls like the mist from a landscape until peace and reason returned..." DEVI

Sherlock Holmes
Plays Foosball

"...The football match does not come within my horizon at all..." MISS

Sherlock Holmes
Visits Pisa

"… not the secret societies of Italy…" STUD

Sherlock Holmes
Cockoo–Clock

"... There was an old clock ticking loudly somewhere in the passage..." ENGI

Sherlock Holmes
As Abe Lincoln

"...An Abraham Lincoln keyed to base uses instead
of high ones would give some idea of the man..."
THOR

Sherlock Holmes Repelling

"…springing over the stones in his way with the activity of a mountain goat…" FINA

Sherlock Holmes
Disguised as Gumby

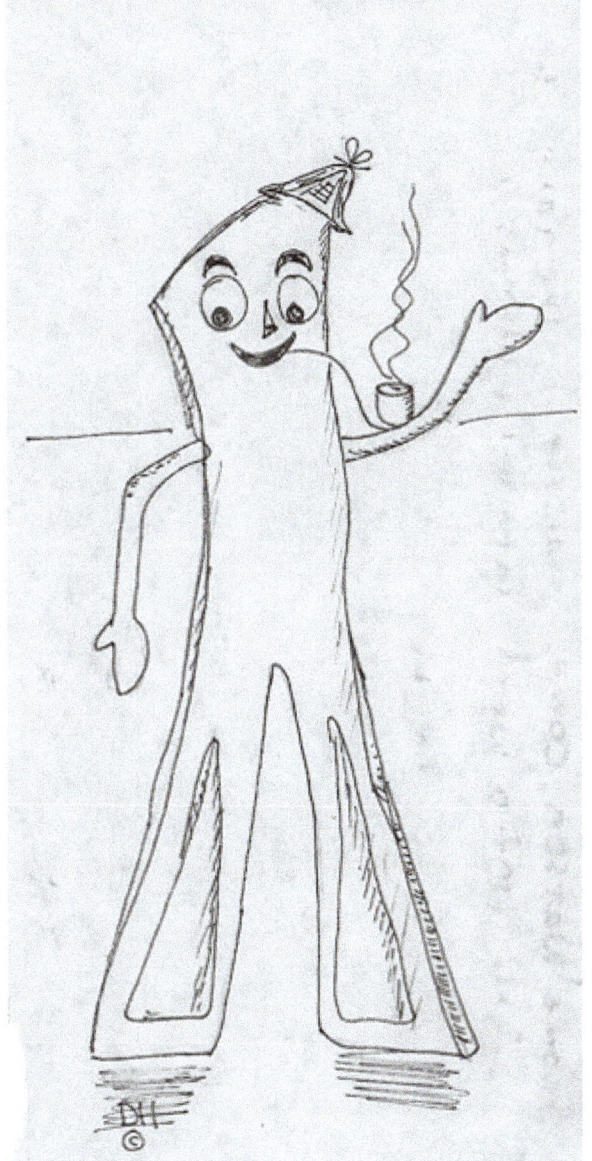

"...the joy which it gave him to be confronted with
this green and gold monster..." GOLD

Sherlock Holmes
Visits Toronto

"...Meyers, Toronto', was printed on the leather inside..." FINA

Sherlock Holmes
Goes Scuba Diving

"...It lay upon a rocky shelf some three feet
under the water..." LION

Sherlock Holmes
At a Disco

"...It is the first Saturday night for seven-and-twenty ears that I have not had my rubber..." FINA

Sherlock Holmes
Visits Kansas

"...John Garrideb, Councellor of Law, Mooreville,
Kansas, USA..." 3Gar

Sherlock Holmes
Celebrates New Years

"...in the New Year week of 1874..." Vall

Sherlock Holmes
And a Lasso

"...How about this rope?" he asked..." RESI

Sherlock Holmes
Takes Yoga

"...I was often weeks on end without putting my foot over the door mat..." REDH

Sherlock Holmes
At Radio City

"...and we are both from New York City..." REDC

Sherlock Holmes Looks
Out His Mid-Town Window

"...He stepped over to the window..." REDH

Sherlock Holmes
Bobble-Head

"...The stout gentleman half rose from his chair and gave a bob of greeting, with a quick little gesturing glance..." REDH

Sherlock Holmes
Moonwalking

"...the figure against the moon..." HOUN

Sherlock Holmes
Gets an X–Ray

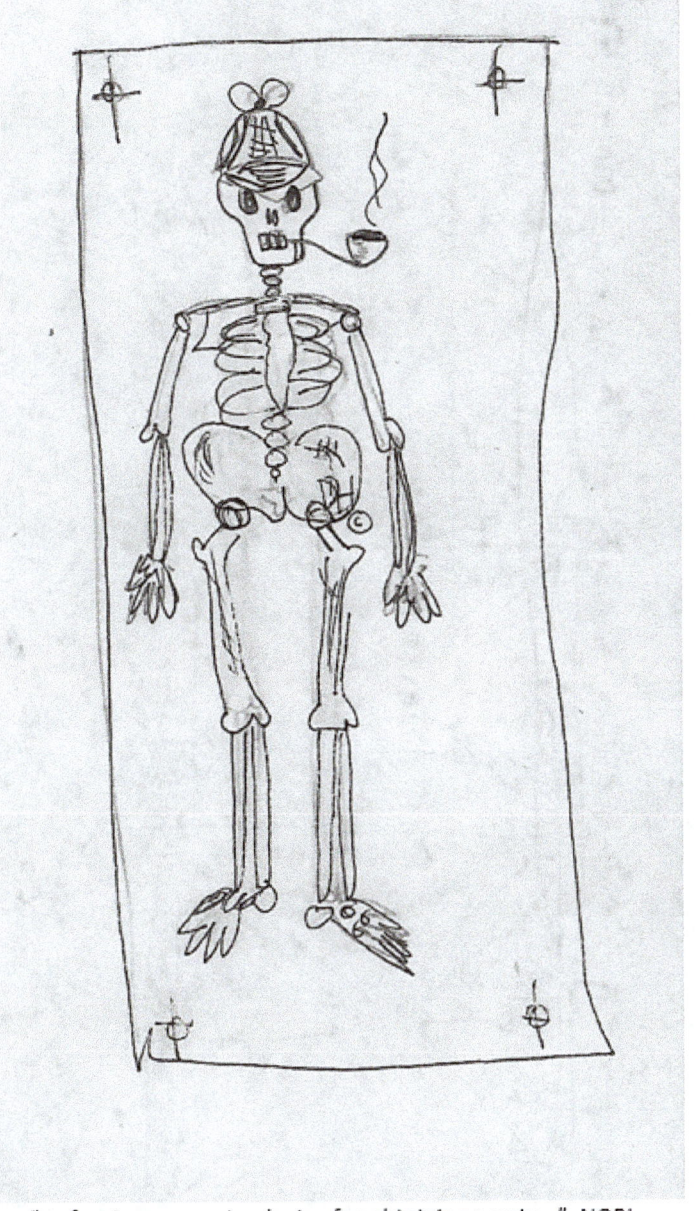

"...of so transparent a device for obtaining a note..." NOBL

Sherlock Holmes Visits
The Sistine Chapel

"...Rome was not built in a day..." STOC

Sherlock Holmes
Fills In For Ringo

"...and with the drumming of a frenzied hand..." MUSG

Sherlock Holmes
Goes Sky–Diving

"...a wisp of green floating in the air caught my eye..."
HOUN

Sherlock Holmes
Cheers the Home Team

"...it was not a cheering prospect..." VALL

Sherlock Holmes
Sweeps a Street

"...well that is a sweeping gerneralization..."   VALL

Sherlock Holmes
Does a Jack–Knife

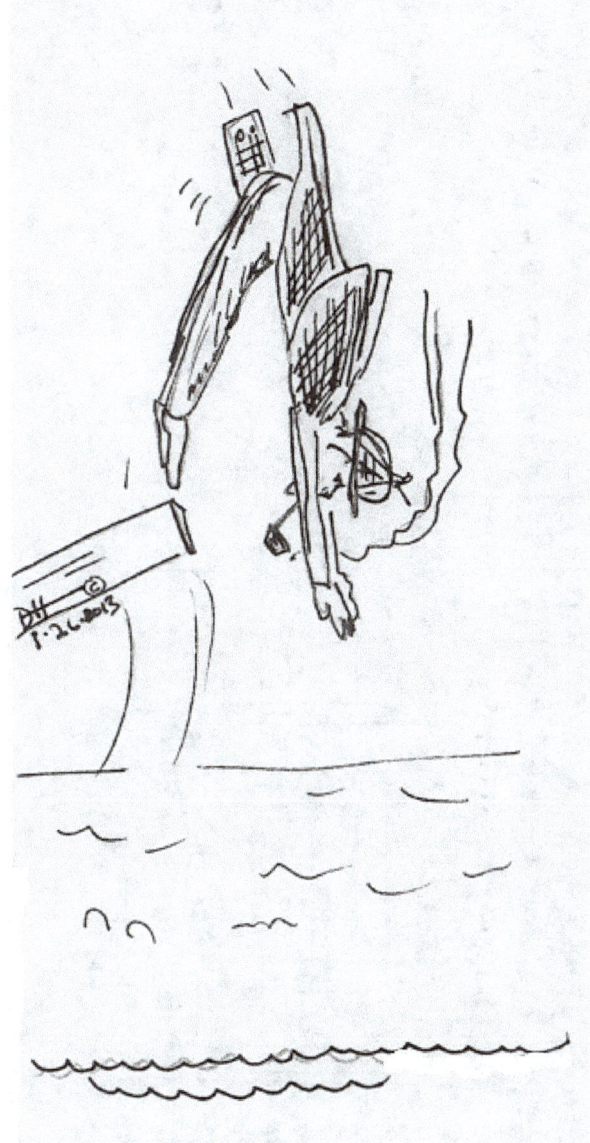

"...and his unanswered correspondence transfixed by a jack-knife..." MUSG

Sherlock Holmes Visits the Statue Of Liberty

"...It is somewhat of a liberty..." GREE

Sherlock Holmes Visits The Trans—America Building

"...in San Fraqncisco, a year ago..."   NOBL

Sherlock Holmes
Does a Head–Stand

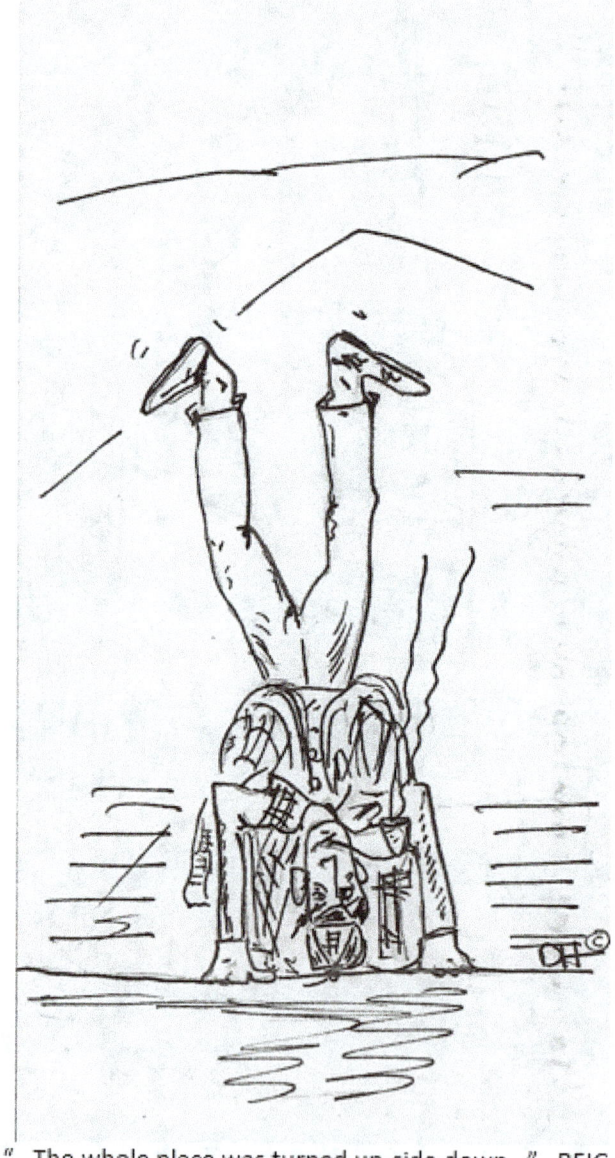

"…The whole place was turned up-side down…"   REIG

Sherlock Holmes and a Saguaro Cactus

"...and then went prospecting in Arizona..."   NOBL

Sherlock Holmes
Hoola–Hooping

"...his hands were raised..." SOLI

Sherlock Holmes
Juggling

"...held his right hand up in the air..."   GOLD

Sherlock Holmes
Flag-Pole Sitting

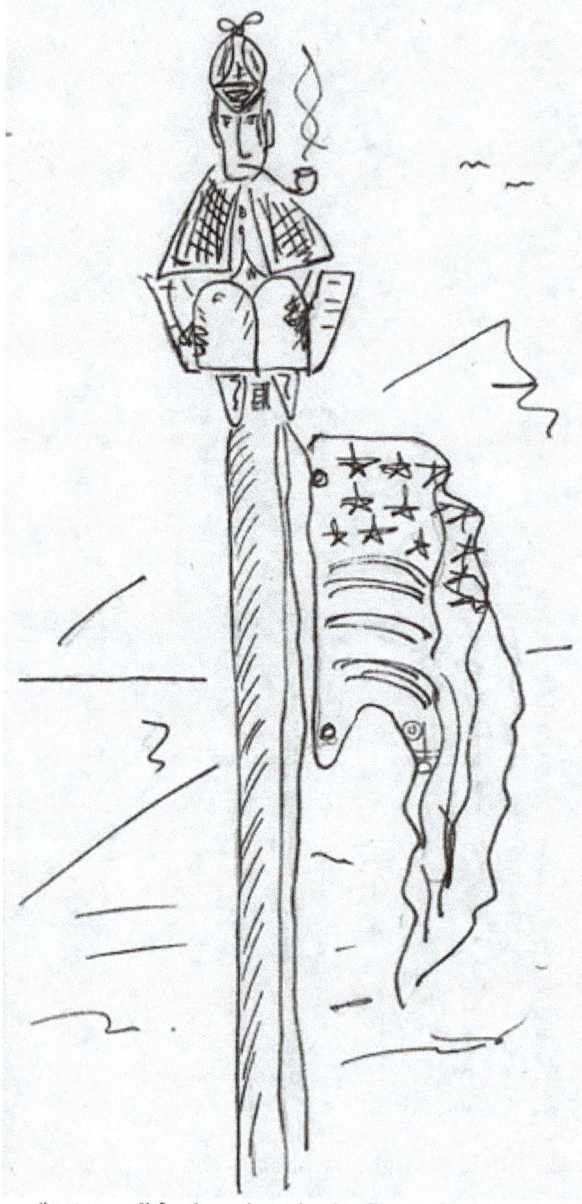

"...You will find me beside the flagstaff..." VALL

Sherlock Holmes
Visits Hawaii

"...and lower the general conditions of life
in this island..."   VALL

Sherlock Holmes Wins the Tour de France

"... Suppose I try my luck upon the bicycle?..."   MISS

Sherlock Holmes at the Coca-Cola Mudseum

"... She went out to America when she was young and lived in the town of Atlanta..."   YELL

Sherlock Holmes
Visits Louisville

"...There are numerous small fry, but few who
would handle so big an affair..."   VALL

Sherlock Holmes
At 221B Sesame Street

"...drove one of the birds, a fine big one..." BLUE

Sherlock Holmes
Enjoys a Milkshake

"...consumed his milk and biscuits..." PRIO

Sherlock Holmes in
A Potato−Sack Race

"...all three armed, and one of them
carrying a sack..."   VALL

Sherlock Holmes
Shot Puts

"...a gigantic ball..." BOSC

Sherlock Holmes
Shows off a Tatoo

"…I made a small study of tatoo marks…" REDH

Sherlock Holmes
Dousing for Water

"...My heart turned to water, for there was no sign of the stone and I knew some terrible mistake had occurred..." BLUE

Sherlock Holmes
Visits Austin

"...But I would rather not talk about the creature, Mr.
Homes, and indeed, he has little to do my story..."
Copp

Sherlock Holmes
Attends the Oscars

"...The credit of the execution is due to Monsieur
Oscar..." EMPT

Sherlock Holmes
Enjoys PEZ

"...and passed her hand over his head with a sweet
womanly caress..." BERY

Sherlock Holmes
Discovers Land

"...well, as you seem to have made a discovery,
whatever it may be..." DEVI

Sherlock Holmes
Visits Antartica

"...It was one bird, I imagine, in which you were
interested — white, with a black bar across
the tail..." BLUE

Sherlock Holmes
Likes Di Vinci

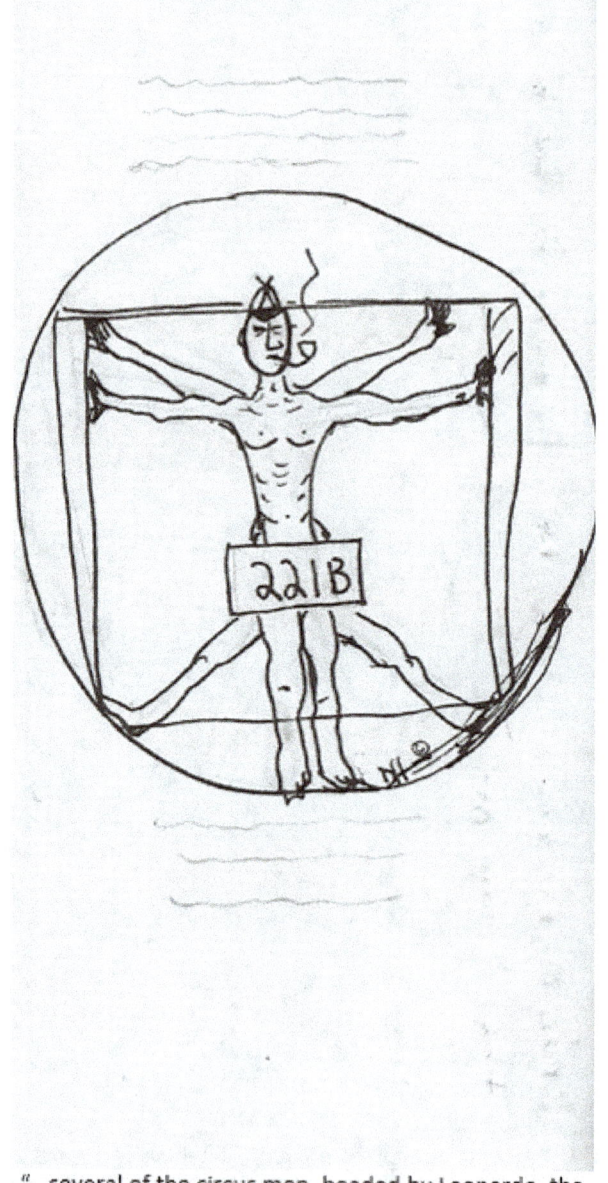

"...several of the circus men, headed by Leonardo, the strong man..." VEIL

Sherlock Holmes
Makes a Short Putt

"...He came on the pretense of playing golf..." BLAC

Sherlock Holmes
Practices Archery

"...and I had written about Abbots and Archery and
Armour..." REDH

Sherlock Holmes
Walks on Stilts

"...looking out, was surpirised to
see his cousin walking very
stealthily..." BERY

Sherlock Holmes
Loves the
Addams Family

"...as he loved his cousin..." Last

Sherlock Holmes
A Tall Tale

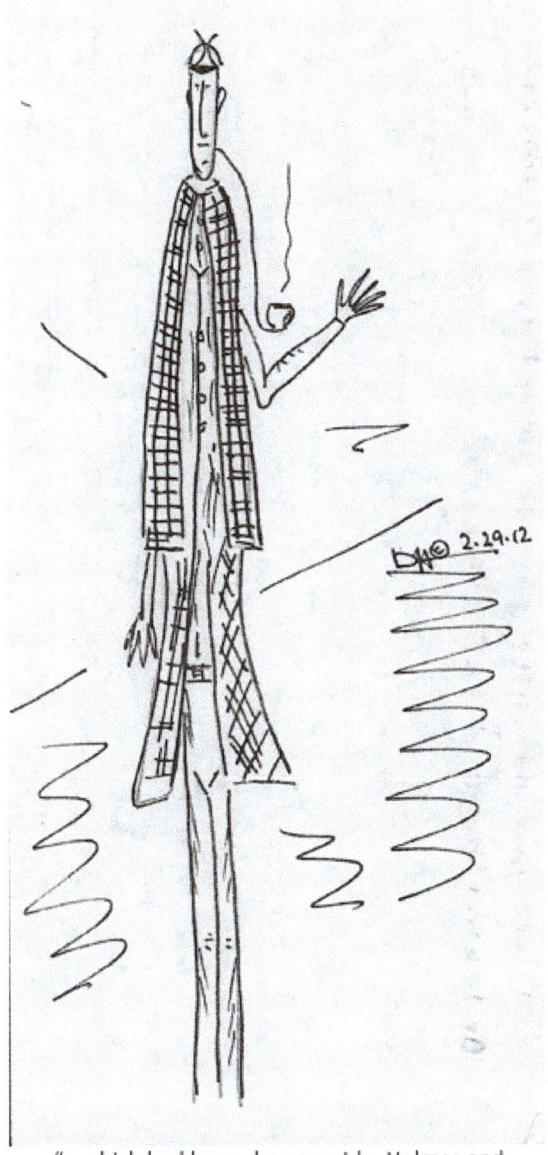

"...which had been drawn out by Holmes and
submitted to the defending counsel..." BOSC

Sherlock Holmes Visits Carlsbad Caverns

"…It is a German speaking country – in Bohemia, not far from Carlsbad…" SCAN

Sherlock Holmes
Disguised as a
Fire Hydrant

"...Holmes sat motionless by the fire..." CHAS

Sherlock Holmes
Visits Iowa

"...It was him that sacked me without a character
on the word of a lying corn..." BOSC

Sherlock Holmes
Visits Birmingham, AL

"...but she died of diptheria while on a visits
to Birmingham..." GLOR

Sherlock Holmes
Visits Easter Island

"...The old peer stared from the stone to the smiling
face before him..." MAZA

Sherlock Holmes
Visits Maine

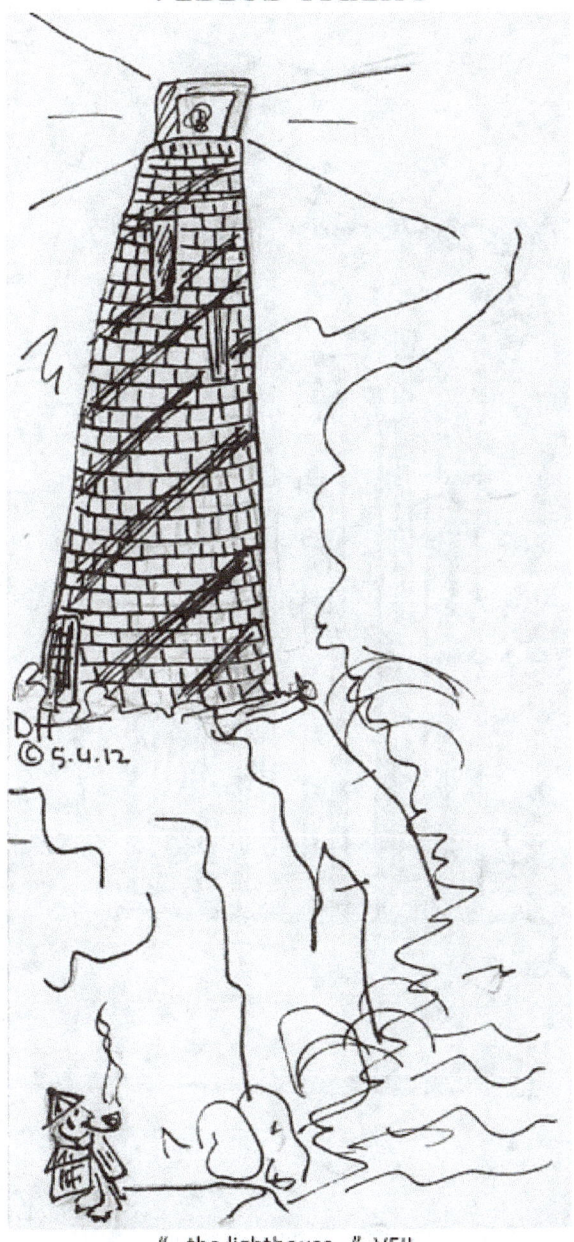

"...the lighthouse..." VEIL

Sherlock Holmes
Meets His Match

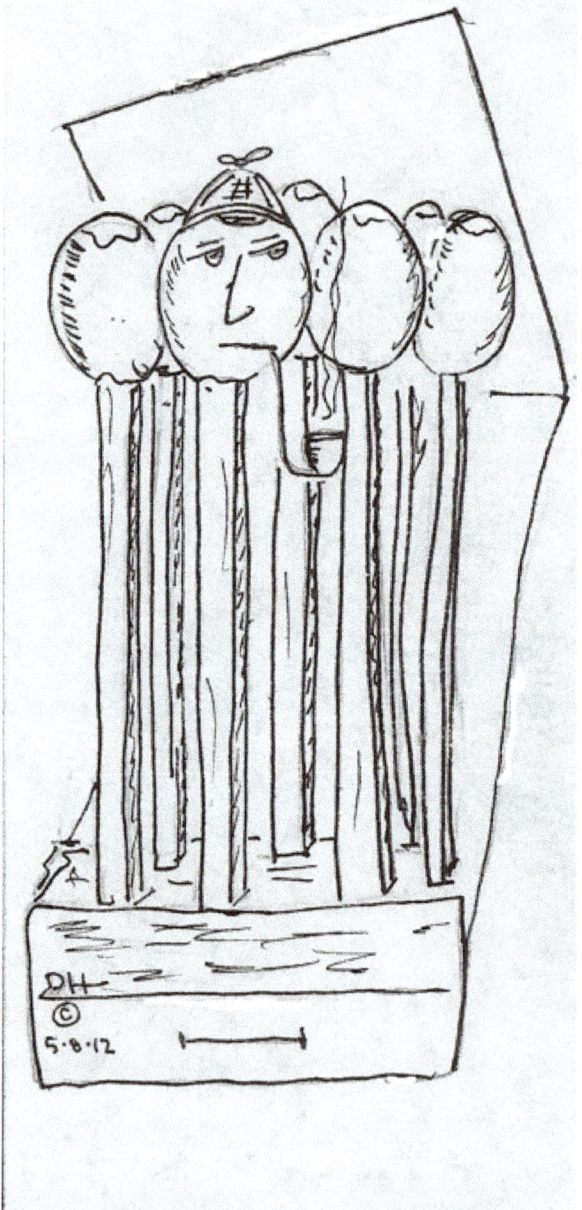

"...Might I trouble you for a match?..." FINA

Sherlock Holmes
Works on His Swing

"...I therefore spent the day at my club..." HOUN

Sherlock Holmes Attends West Point Graduation

"...He was a tall, dark, heavy moustached, rather military-looking man..." RETI

Sherlock Holmes
Visits Yankton, SD

"...Because I knew it was nowhere else..." SECO

Sherlock Holmes
On the Horizonal Bar

"...Holmes cut the cord and removed the transverse bar..." CARD

Sherlock Holmes Visits Pamplona

"...The little monster was as strong as a bull..." BLAN

Sherlock Holmes at Barcelona Oylmpic Stadium

"...to the tower. Tell them to stop opposite Jacob's yard..." SIGN

Sherlock Holmes
Cocks–Up

"…with the sign of a game-cock above the door…"
PRIO

Sherlock Holmes as the Symbol of Madrid

"...won't ber much strain..." MUSG

Sherlock Holmes Watches 'A Christmas Story'

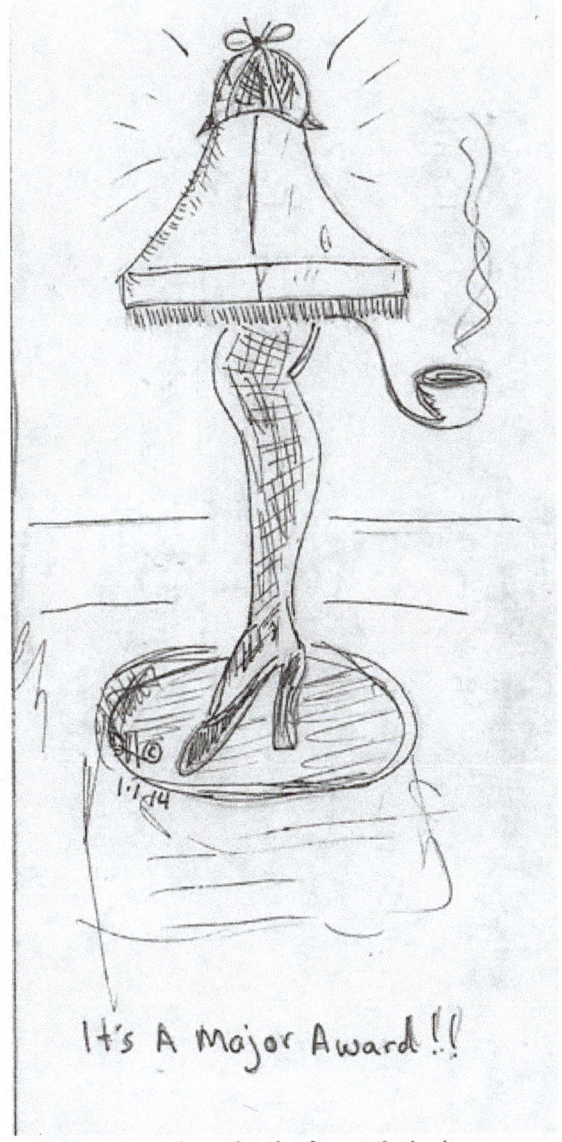

It's A Major Award!!

"...Then I sat down by the fire with the lamp on a table beside me....however by Ralph..." BLAN

Sherlock Holmes in a 10-Gallon Deerstalker

"...Holmes took his hat and shrugged his shoulders..."
ABBE

Sherlock Holmes
At the Zoo

"...Looking between the branches we saw the tall,
erect figure emerge..." CREE

Sherlock Holmes With Pin-Point Pupils

"...drooping eye lids, and pin-pointed pupils..." TWIS

Sherlock Holmes
Saddles Up

"...dabbled with white froth, went past with traveling
bridle and empty saddle..." HOUN

Sherlock Holmes
Gets to the Bottom

"...and then diving down..." REDH

Sherlock Holmes
Getting Tiki with It

"...the lovely, distant island..." VALL

Sherlock Holmes
Enjoys Mardi Gras

"...and Samson of New Orleans..." STUD

Sherlock Holmes
Armours Up

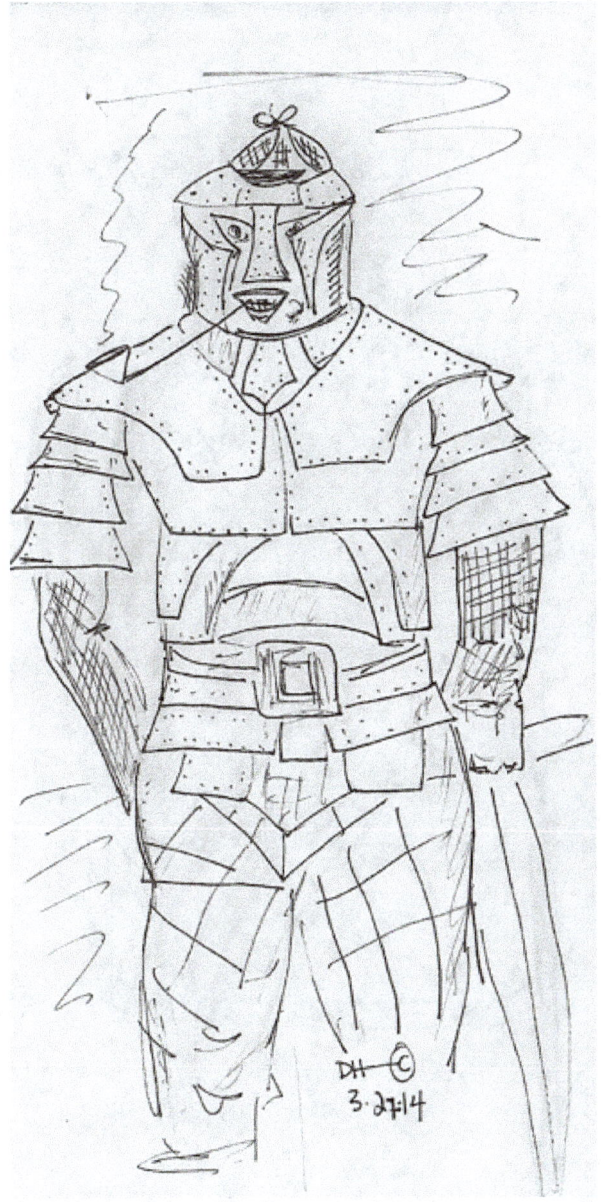

"...and what seemed to be a suit of Japanese armour..."
GREE

Sherlock Holmes
Flies Commercial

"...packed all the eatibles he could find..." STUD

Sherlock Holmes on a Trampoline (again)

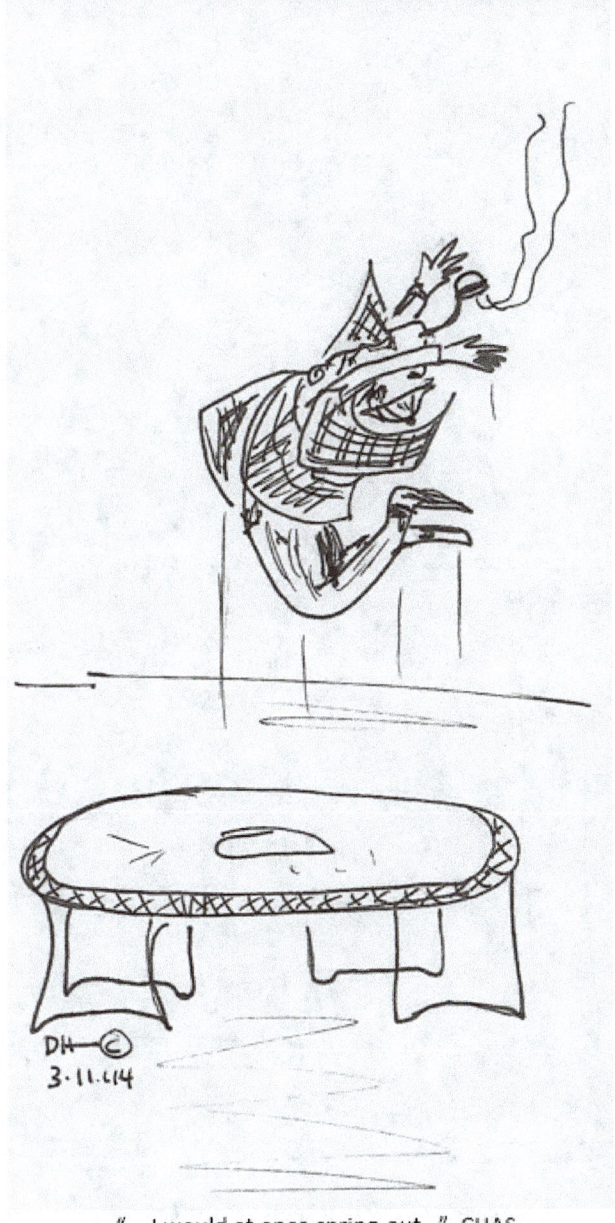

"... I would at once spring-out..." CHAS

Sherlock Holmes
In a Penguin Suit

"... He was so furred to keep out the cold..." VALL

Sherlock Holmes
Plays above the Rim

"...then he clambered up to the rim..." SILV

Sherlock Holmes
Visits IHOP

"...I came down to breakfast in the morning..." BERY

Sherlock Holmes
Digs the ʻStones

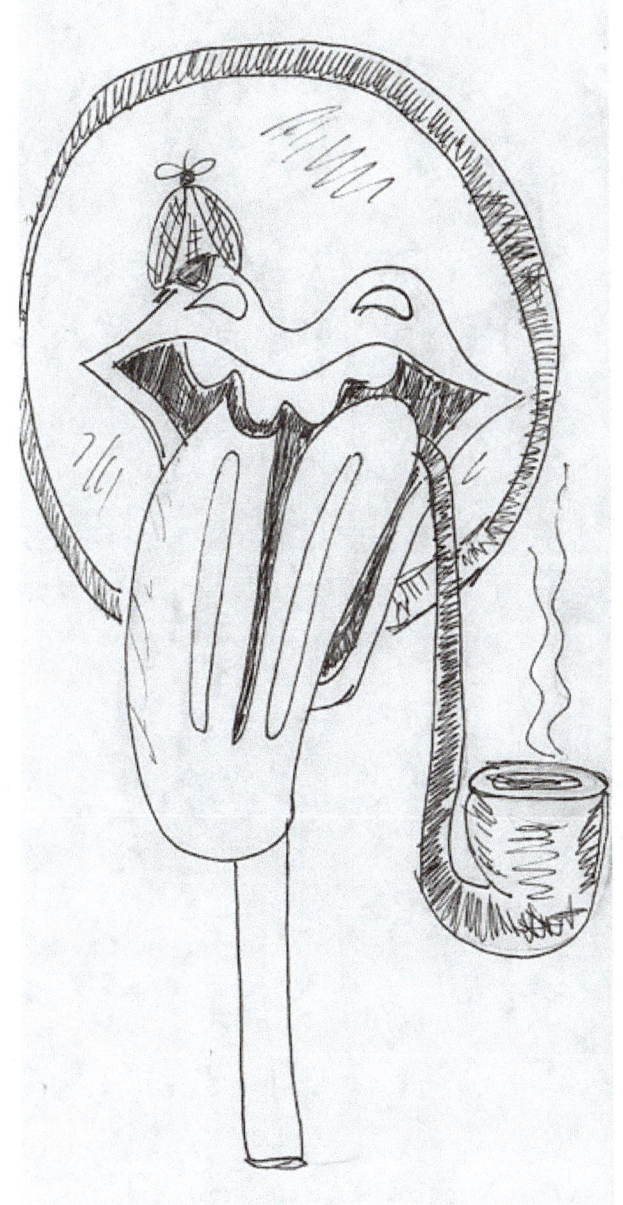

"...upon my lip..." Empt

Sherlock Holmes
Has Some Pi

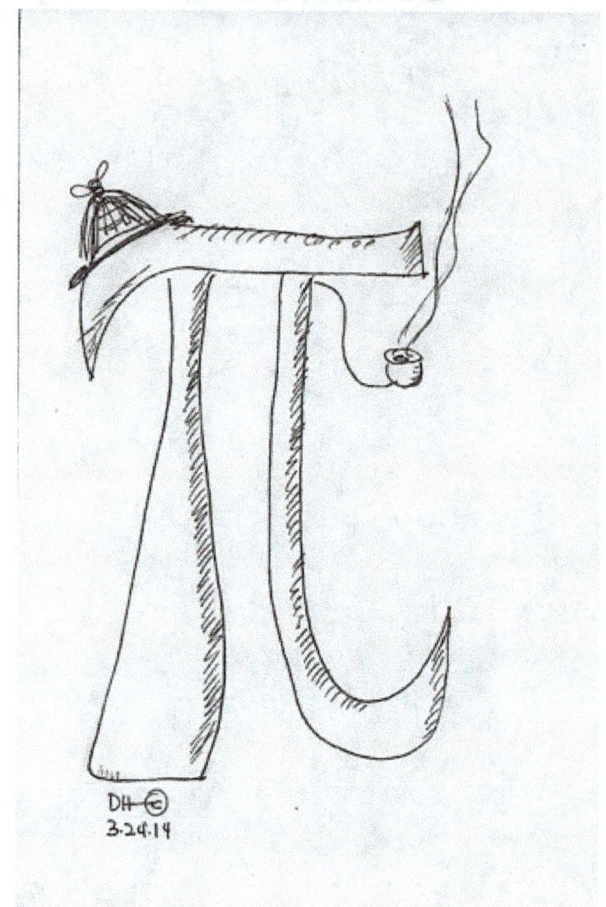

"…There were a couple of brace of cold woodcock, a
pheasant, a *pâté de foie gras pie*…" NOBL

Sherlock Holmes
Watches The Godfather

ᵛ"...His head had been shattered by a savage blow..." SILV

Sherlock Holmes Has
The Best Office Gossip

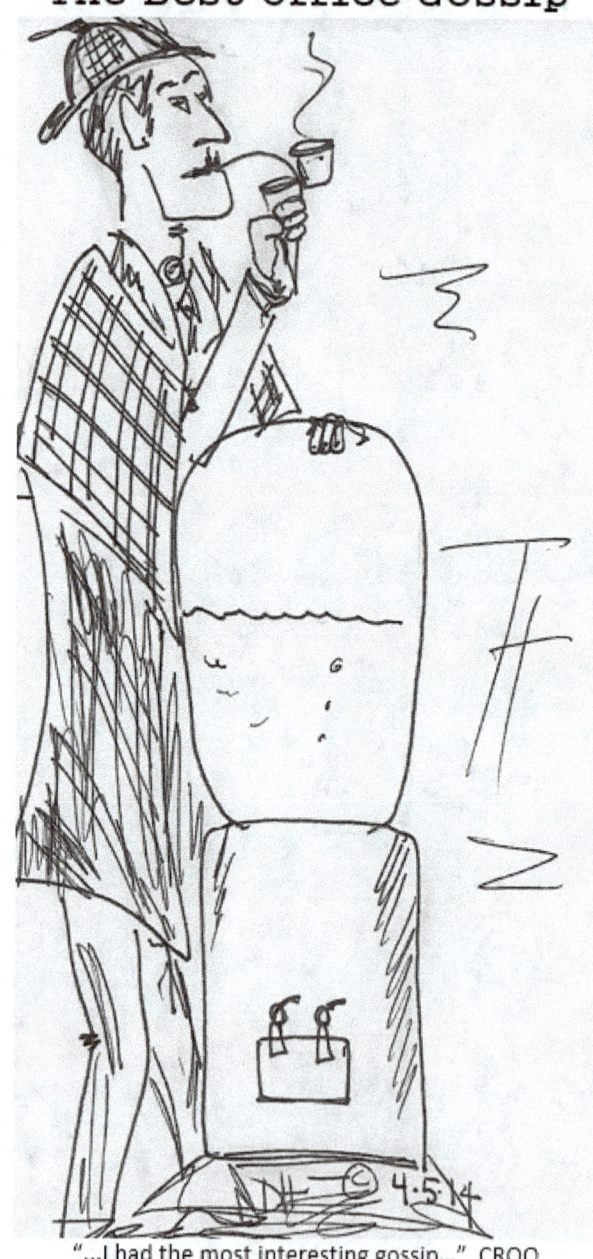

"...I had the most interesting gossip..." CROO

Sherlock Holmes
Enjoys another Easter

"...and a little wizened man darted out of it, like a rabbit..." NORW

Sherlock Holmes
At Buc-ee's

"...He should have been a Buck in the days of the regency..." SHOS

Sherlock Holmes
Fashion Icon

"…the earring…" CARD

Sherlock Holmes
Discovers a Donut Tree

"...The Origin of the Tree Worship..." EMPT

Sherlock Holmes
Enjoys a Pinot Noir

"...Now you must have some wine..." TWIS

Sherlock Holmes
Plays a Stratocaster

"...an old-fashioned pinfire revolver, and a guitar
were among the personal property..." WIST

Sherlock Holmes
Relates to Dilbert

"...he was at home the whole of Monday after office
hours..." BRUC

Sherlock Holmes
Attends the U.S. Open

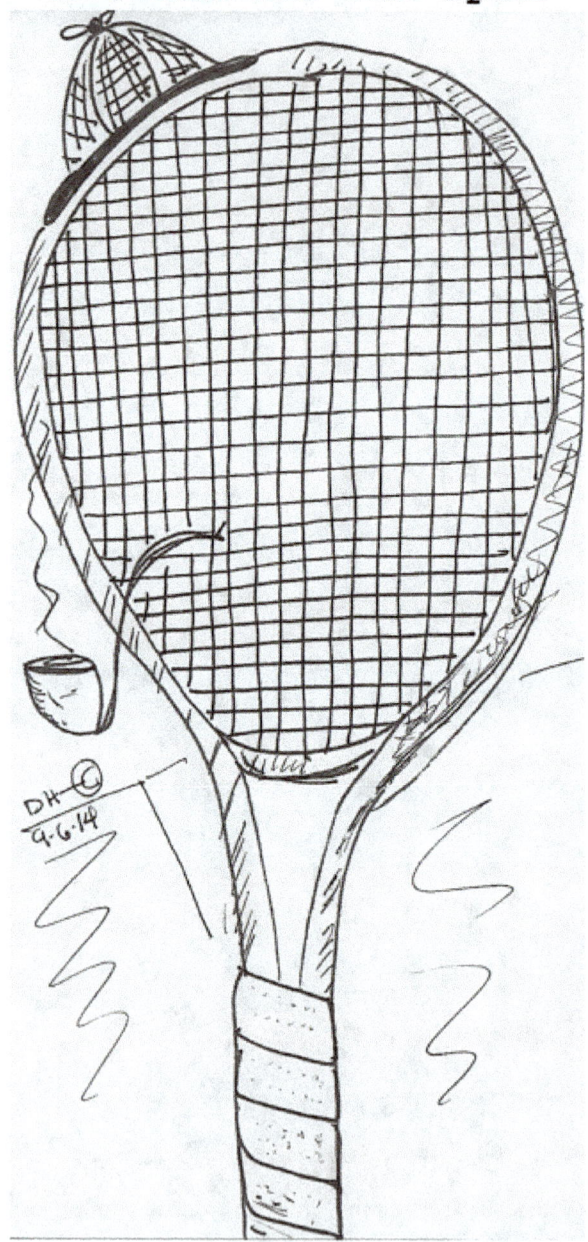

"...I have rubber-soled tennis shoes..." CHAS

Sherlock Holmes
Read Playboy Once

"...What woman could ever be worthy of such a man..."
REDC

Sherlock Holmes
Cracks a Hardboil Case

"...much the worst for the wear and cracked in several places..." BLUE

Sherlock Holmes
Attends the State Fair
Of Texas

"...It was the body of a tall, well-made man..." ABBE

Sherlock Holmes
Another Capital Idea

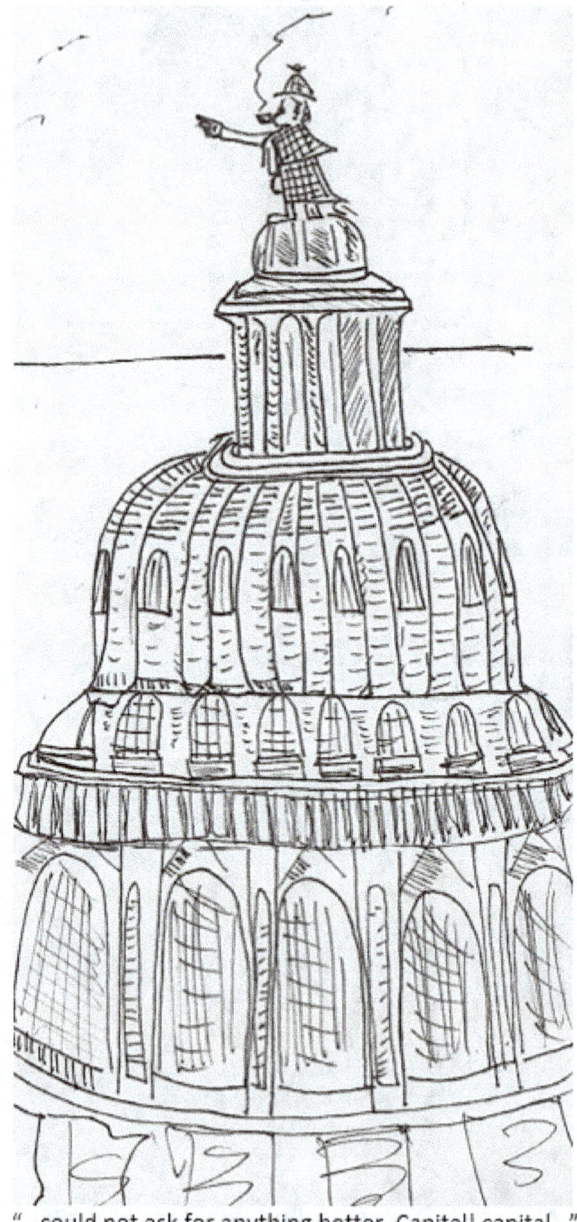

"...could not ask for anything better. Capital! capital..."
COPP

Sherlock Holmes
Visits Philadelphia

"...sounds as a bell..." MISS

Sherlock Holmes
Is a Barrel of Fun

"...We were given a suit of a sailor togs each,
a barrel of water,..." GLOR

Sherlock Holmes
Has a Good Idea

"...Oh, that's your idea..." ILLU

Sherlock Holmes
Disguised as Pinocchio

"...who he met in the wood, that his mother longed
to see him..." PRIO

Sherlock Holmes Saves 15% with GEICO

"...the most winning woman I ever knew was hanged for poisoning three little children for their insurance-money..." VALL

Sherlock Holmes Re-enacts "A Christmas Story"

"...The founder of that great emporium proved to be a brisk, crisp little person, very dapper and quick, with a clear head and a quick tongue..."
SIXN

Sherlock Holmes Is
Deiced Before Takeoff

"...the icy coolness..." 3GAB

Sherlock Holmes
Lost in Thought

"...lost in profound thought..." ABBE

Sherlock Holmes
Meets Georgia O'Keefe

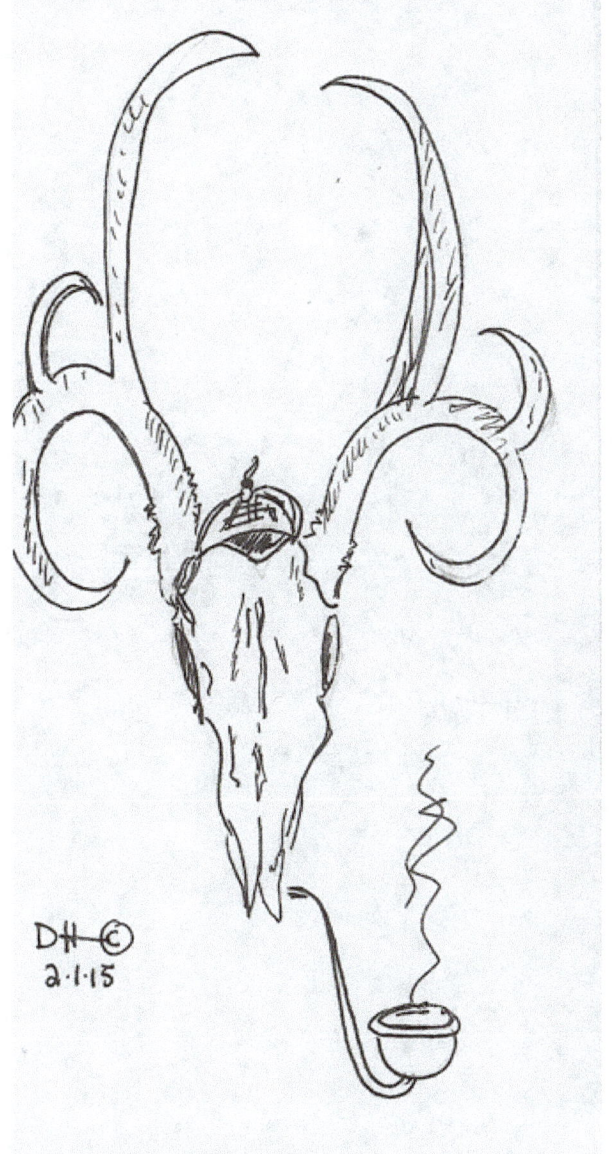

"…Yes, Sir. But he was off like a deer…" REIG

Sherlock Holmes Disguised as the Maltese Falcon

"...statue upon his pedestal..." HOUN

Sherlock Holmes Meets the Headless Horseman

"...Whenever a horseman clattered down the road..."
STUD

Sherlock Holmes
Wears Crocs

"...A crocodile took me just as I was half-way across
and nipped off my right leg..." SIGN

Sherlock Holmes as an Blow–Up Advetisment

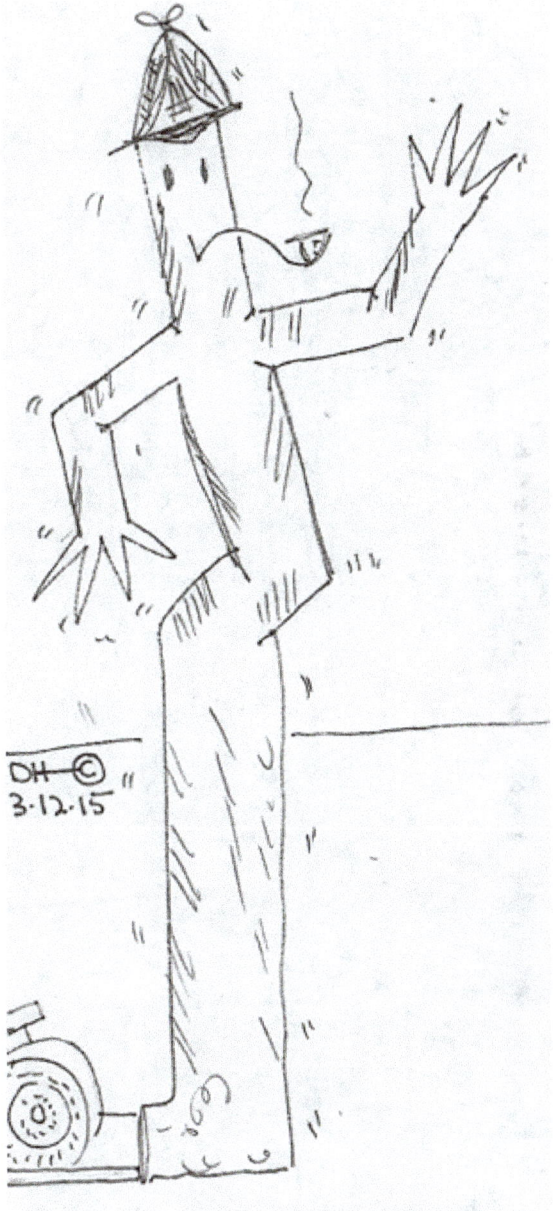

"...Their blow fell -- or his blow..." ILLU

Sherlock Holmes
Maître'd

"...and they had drawn a bottle of wine which stood there..." ABBE

Sherlock Holmes Likes The Traveling Man Sculpture

Deep Ellum
Dallas, Tx

"...This pretended merchant, who travels under
the name of Achmet..." SIGN

Sherlock Holmes
Is a Deadhead

BLUESFORALLAH

"...a skeleton with a tangle of brown hair..." HOUN

Sherlock Holmes
May 4th Be With Him

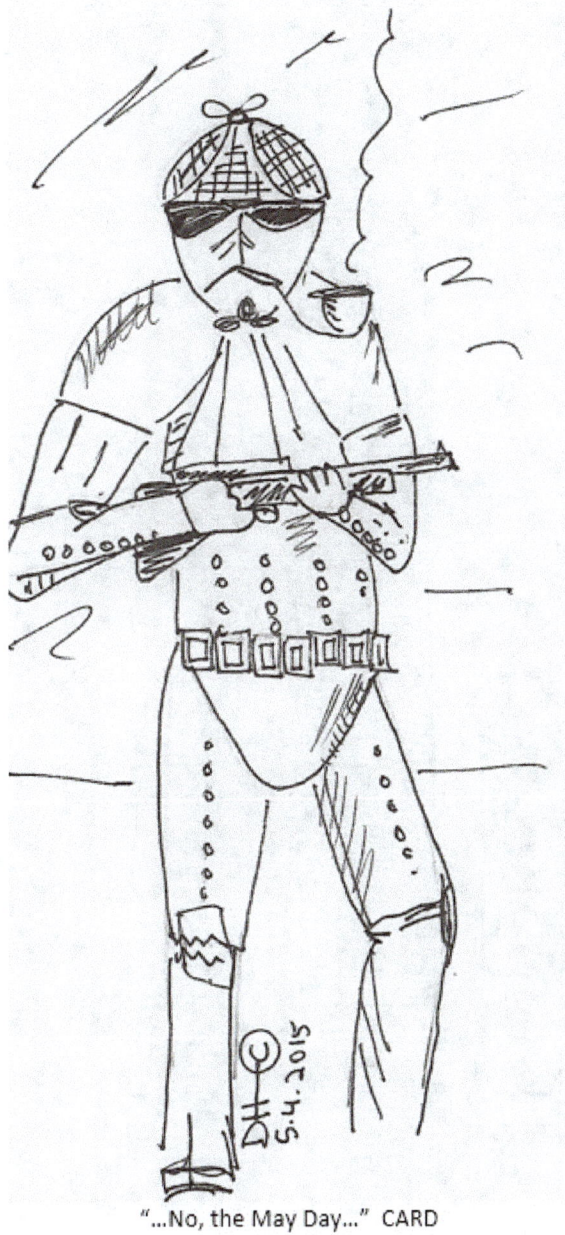

"...No, the May Day..." CARD

Sherlock Holmes
Visits One
World Trade Center

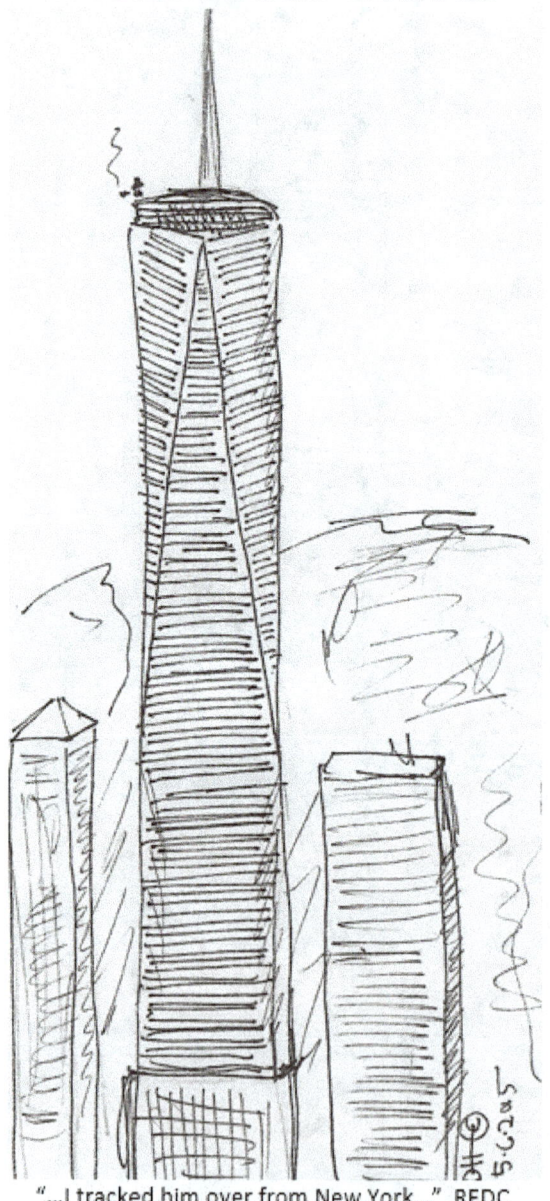

"...I tracked him over from New York..." REDC

Sherlock Holmes
Loves David Letterman

"...When our host returned it was clear from his downcast face that he had made no progress..." ILLU

Sherlock Holmes at The Sam Houston Statue

"...You've given the govenor such a turn..." GLOR

Sherlock Holmes
Visits Texas
May 2015

"...Mr. Soames was somewhat over whelmed by
this flood..." 3STU

Sherlock Holmes
Disguised as a
Carved Coconut

"...leaving no traces upon the coconut matting..."
GOLD

Sherlock Holmes
Is Saddened by
Hate Crimes

"...I know that I hate it..." DYIN

Sherlock Holmes
Soars Like an Eagle

"...like some wondering eagle..." LAST

Sherlock Holmes Celebrates July 4th

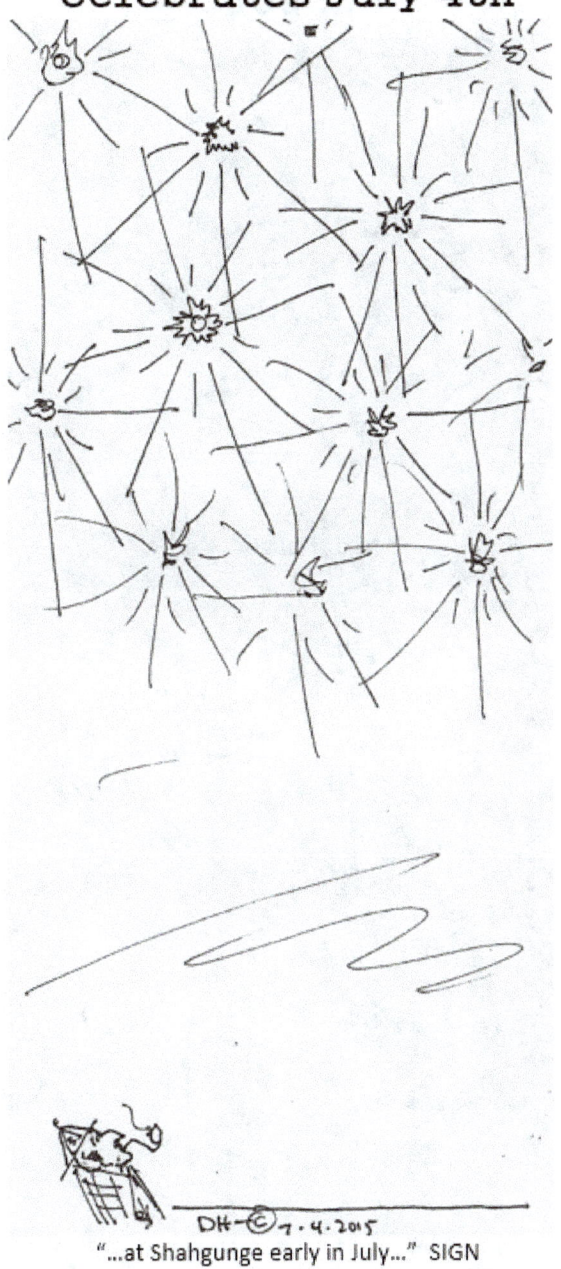

DH—© 7·4·2015

"...at Shahgunge early in July..." SIGN

Sherlock Holmes
Supports
Same Sex Marriage

"...but if you persist in this marriage you will raise
up a swarm of powerful enemies..." ILLU

Sherlock Holmes Re-wears His 10-Gallon Deerstalker

"...and a large, red feather in a broad-brimmed hat..."
IDEN

Sherlock Holmes
Visits El Paso

"...When I glanced again, his face had resumed that red-indian composure..." CROO

Sherlock Holmes Enters a Soap-Box Derby

"...Sir Robert has got to win this derby..." SHOS

Sherlock Holmes
Goes Rock Climbing

"...sure of foot and firm grip, climbing apparently in
mere joy at his own powers..." CREE

Sherlock Holmes
Plays Flamingo Guitar

"...a pink feather from some gigantic flamingo..." SIGN

Sherlock Holmes
At a Nudist Camp

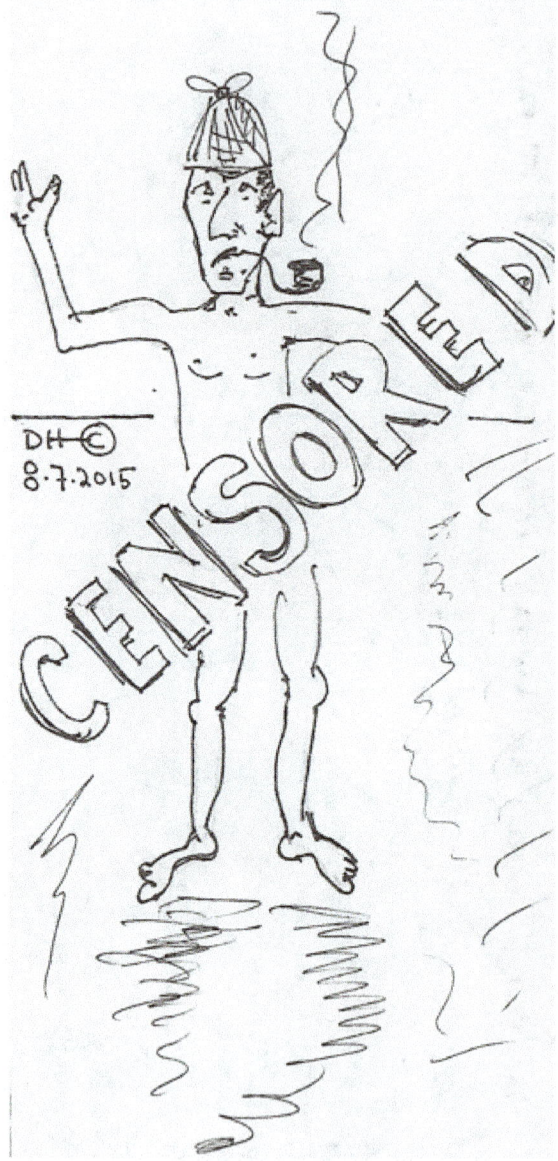

"...which I saw with delight belonged to a man with naked feet..." BERY

Sherlock Holmes On
The Brooklyn Bridge

"...in Brooklyn..." REDC

Sherlock Holmes
Loved the 60's

"...if you can enjoy it in peace, well and good..." FIVE

Sherlock Holmes
Chimney Sweeping

"...was it through the chimney?..." SIGN

Sherlock Holmes
Reads Maurice Sendak

"...as strange as a wild beast..." BLAC

Sherlock Holmes
On the Spanish Steps

"...He was Attaché at Rome, and he died there..."
3GAB

Sherlock Holmes
Perfers Fountain Pens

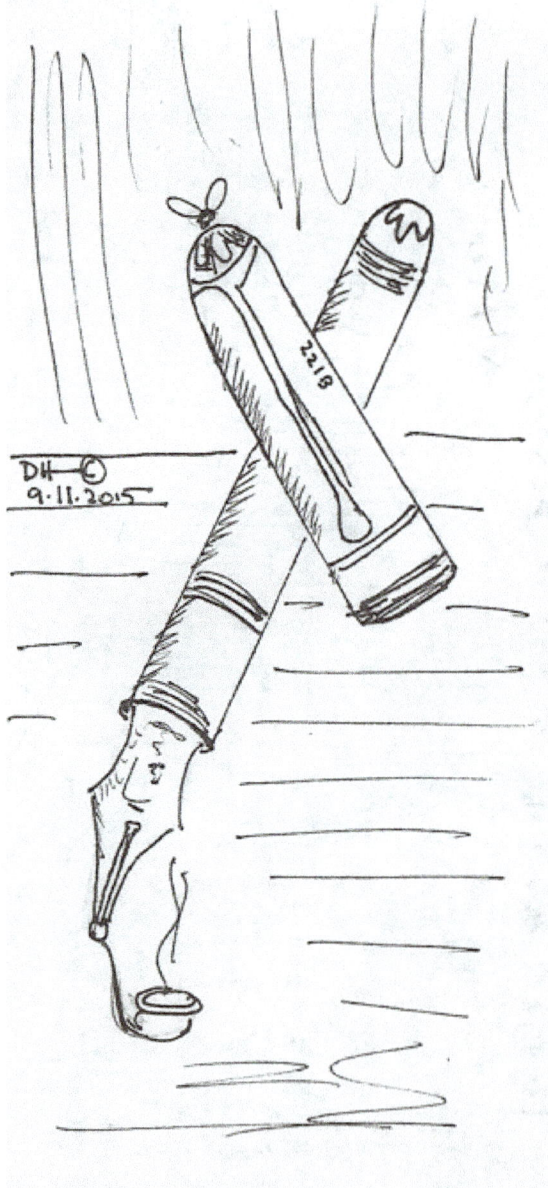

"...It was done by a thick pen..." VALL

Sherlock Holmes
Enjoys Some Cava

"...It is good wine, Holmes..." LAST

Sherlock Holmes
Sherlock Holmes at
Galata Tower Istanbul

"...The one with the corner tower and slate roof..."
LION

Sherlock Holmes
Cleans Up

"...you have some reason for washing your hands..." STUD

Sherlock Holmes
Enjoys Swan Lake

"...The new dance was in this form..." DANC

Sherlock Holmes Crosses the Road

"...She is just a stray chicken in the world of foxes..."
LADY

Sherlock Holmes
Watches Godzilla

"...he was brought down for destruction..." VALL

Sherlock Holmes
Gets Pumped-Up

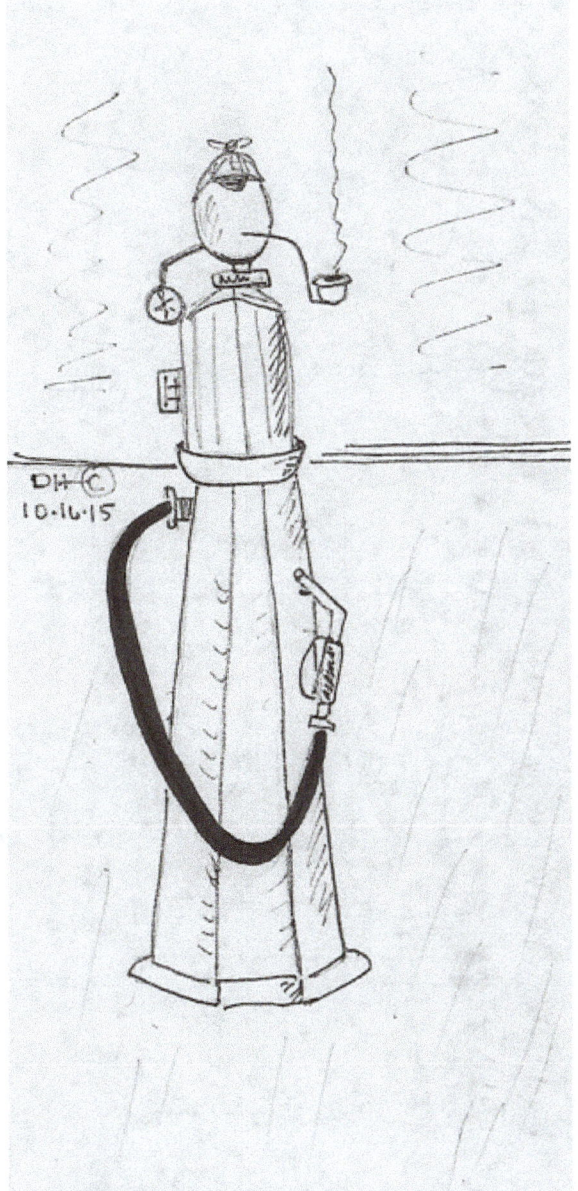

"...If he talks of a radiator, it is a battleship, of an
oil pump a cruiser, and so on..." LAST

Sherlock Holmes
Samples His Ragu

"…Five years – when I should have a medal the size of
a soup-plate…" 3GAR

Sherlock Holmes
Disguised As a
Black–Eyed Pea

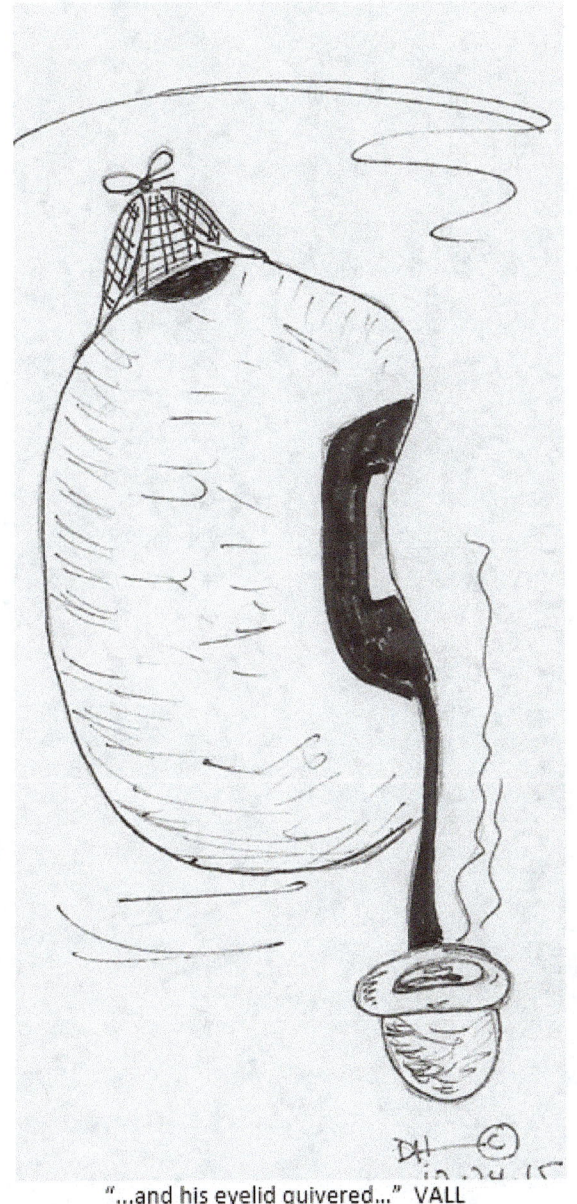

"...and his eyelid quivered..." VALL

Sherlock Holmes
Never Inhales

"...I did not breathe freely..." BERY

Sherlock Holmes
Visits Cleveland

ROCK AND ROLL
HALL OF FAME + MUSEUM

"...well, well, such is fame..." EMPT

Sherlock Holmes
At the Hope Bridge

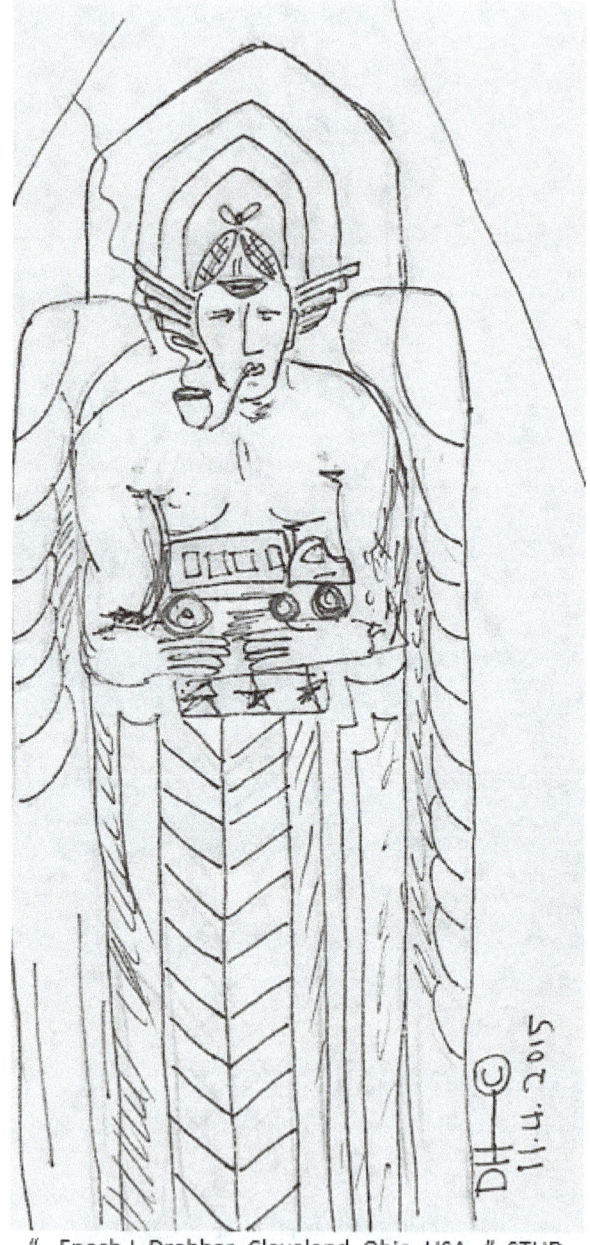

"...Enoch J. Drebber, Cleveland, Ohio, USA..." STUD

Sherlock Holmes
Is Always Top Banana

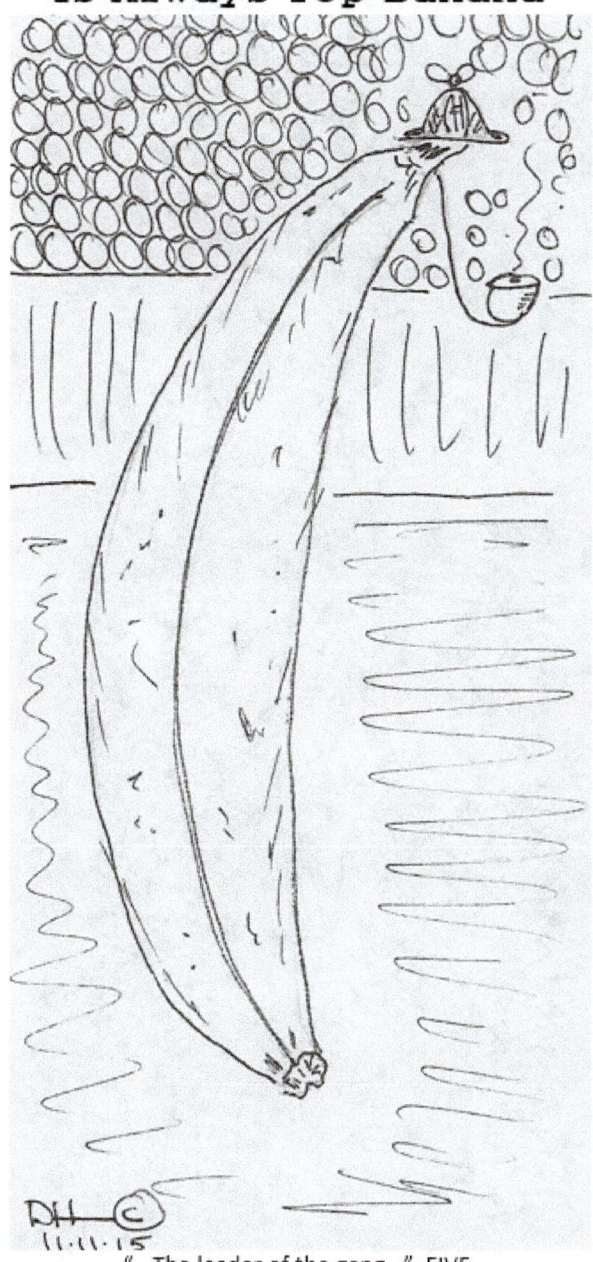

"...The leader of the gang..." FIVE

Sherlock Holmes
Remebers the Field
Of Flanders

"...I was overwhelmed by the honour..." BERY

Sherlock Holmes
Plays Jimi Hendrix

"...Is a tall man, left-handed, limps with the right..." BOSC

Sherlock Holmes
Uses an Ice–Pick

"...but only to pick them up..." SILV

Sherlock Holmes Returns to Kansas

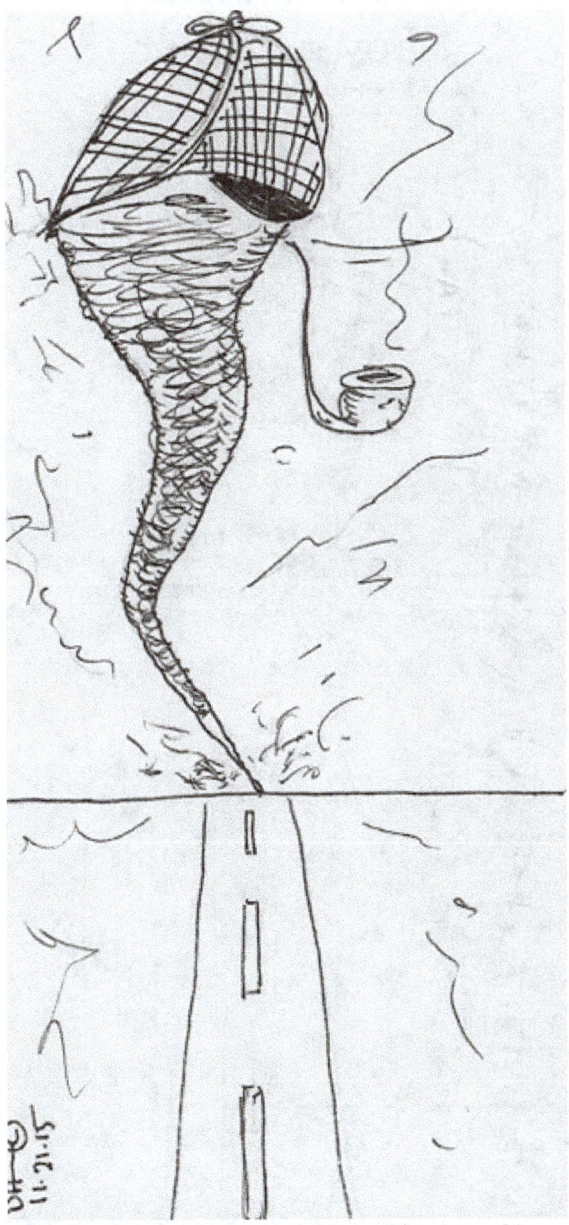

"...If you came from Kansas I would not need to
explain to you..." 3GAR

Sherlock Holmes
Attends the
Macy's Parade

"...they walked along the Parade..." CARD

Sherlock Holmes
Feeling Melancholy

"...The man in the dressing-gown turned upon us
with a most melancholy face..." SIXN

Sherlock Holmes
Is Never Frosty

"...and remote as a snow image..." ILLU

Sherlock Holmes
Ornamentally

"...I have said that a decoration of yew trees circled the garden..." VALL

Sherlock Holmes
Misses John Lennon

"...you who love me..." GLOR

Sherlock Holmes
Disavows Darth Vader

"...it is very clear we have traced the evil back to its source..." CREE

Sherlock Holmes
Remembers Ravi Shankar

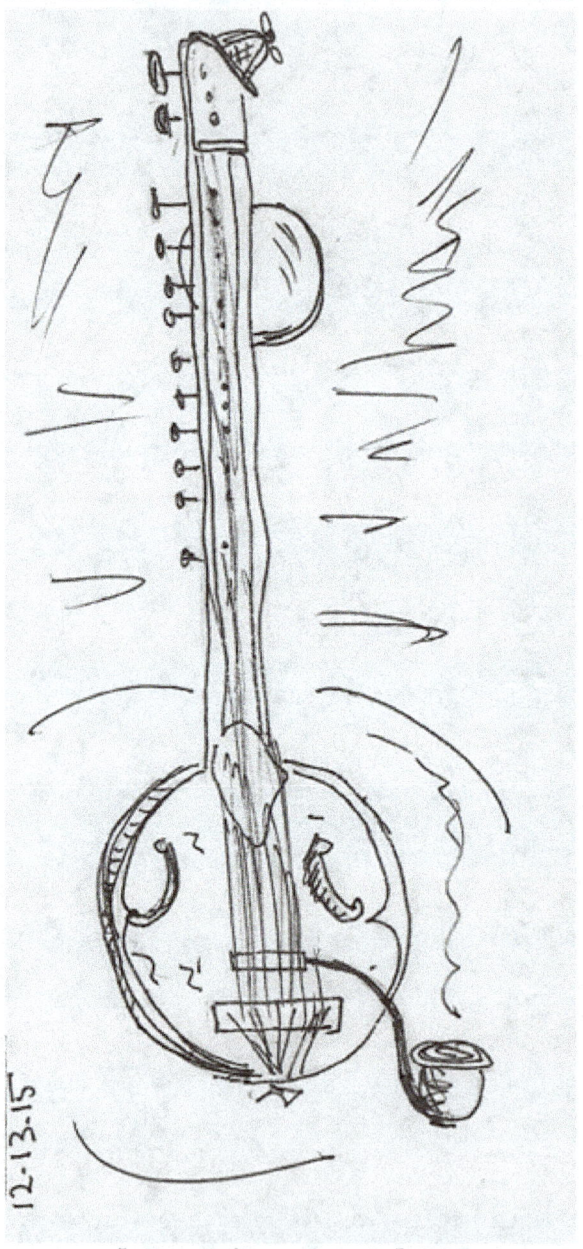

"...In an Indian regiment..." SIGN

Sherlock Holmes
Admires Picasso

"...To the man who loves art for its own sake..." COPP

Sherlock Holmes
Disguised A a Minion

"...tracked his enemies from city to city. Working his
way in any minial capacity..." STUD

Sherlock Holmes
Rings the In New Year

"...we were to marry at the New Year..." BRUC

Sherlock Holmes
One Direction

"...But all I heard pointed in the one direction..." BLAC

Sherlock Holmes
Visits Washington

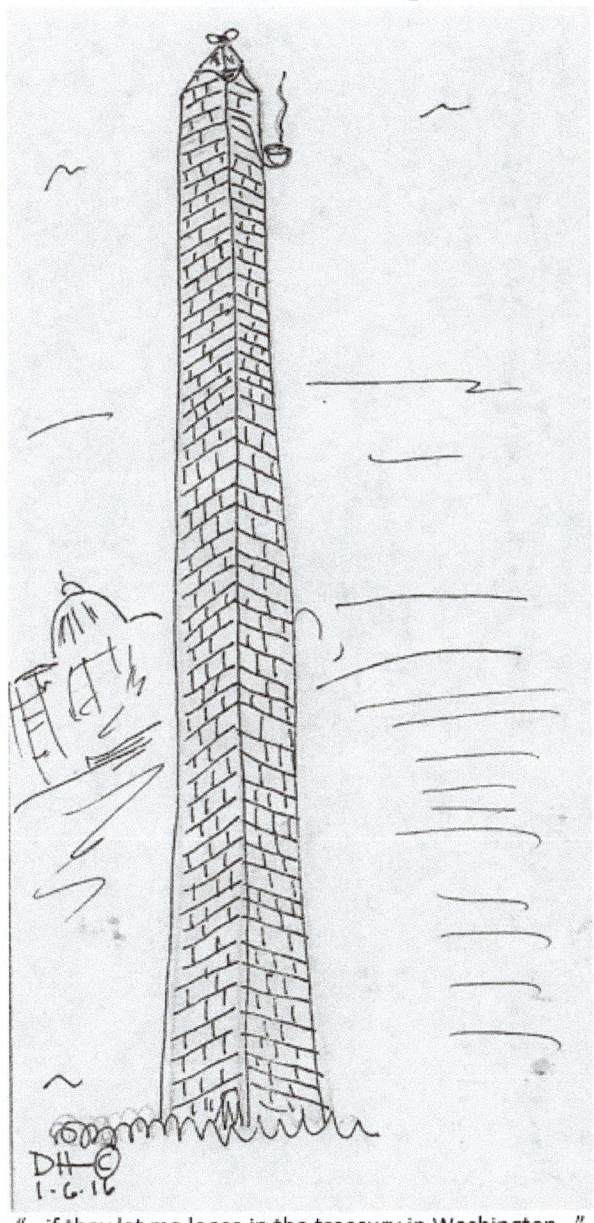

"...if they let me loose in the treasury in Washington..."
VALL

Sherlock Holmes
Attends the Super Bowl

"...to the great bowl..." SIGN

Sherlock Holmes
Drives a Bus

"...I came round as quickly as the Bayswater bus would bring me..." MISS

Sherlock Holmes
Studies Ventriloquism

"...the strange dummy ..." EMPT

Sherlock Holmes
Frayed Knot

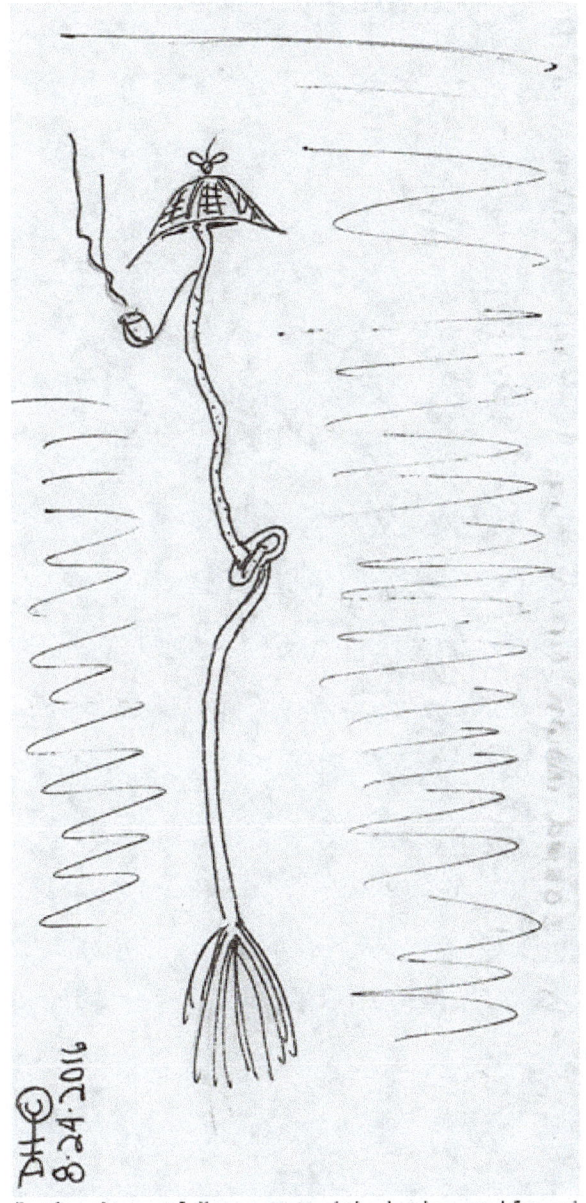

"...Then he carefully scrutinized the broken and frayed
end where it had snapped off ..." ABBE

Sherlock Holmes
Opens a Can of Worms

"...Why does fate play such tricks with poor, helpless worms? ..." BOSC

Sherlock Holmes
Controls the Remote

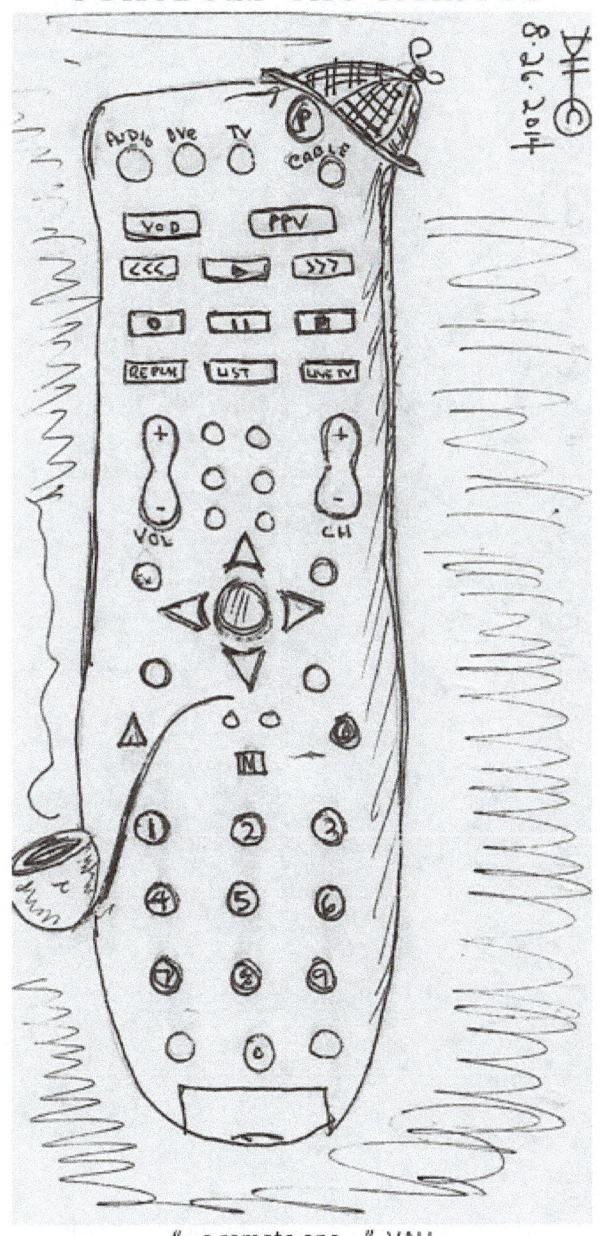

"...a remote one ..." VALL

Sherlock Holmes
Likes Willie Wonka

"...at the end of that time, I emerged with a little chocolate ..." LION

Sherlock Holmes
Visits Cortona

"...which can only be descended by single, long, tortuous path, which is steep and slippery ..." LION

Sherlock Holmes
Like the Dallas Cowboys
Cheerleaders

"...I tried to cheer him up by wire ..." MISS

Sherlock Holmes
Enjoys a Fletcher's
Corn–Dog

"...he has had a fair price..." LADY

Sherlock Holmes
Sees a Radiologist

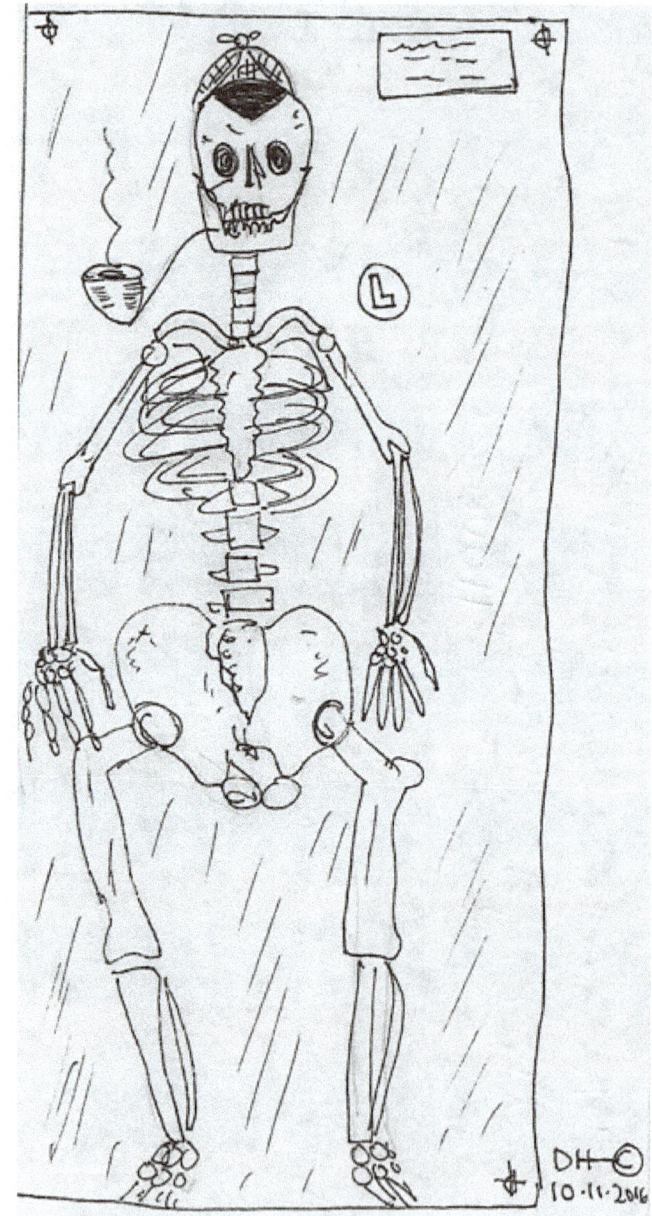

"...hardly more fleshy than that of a skeleton..." STUD

Sherlock Holmes
Skates in Holland

"...It was from the reigning family of Holland..." IDEN

Sherlock Holmes
Likes Houdini

"...his gold chains more weighty across a more gorgeous vest..." LADY

Sherlock Holmes
iPhone App

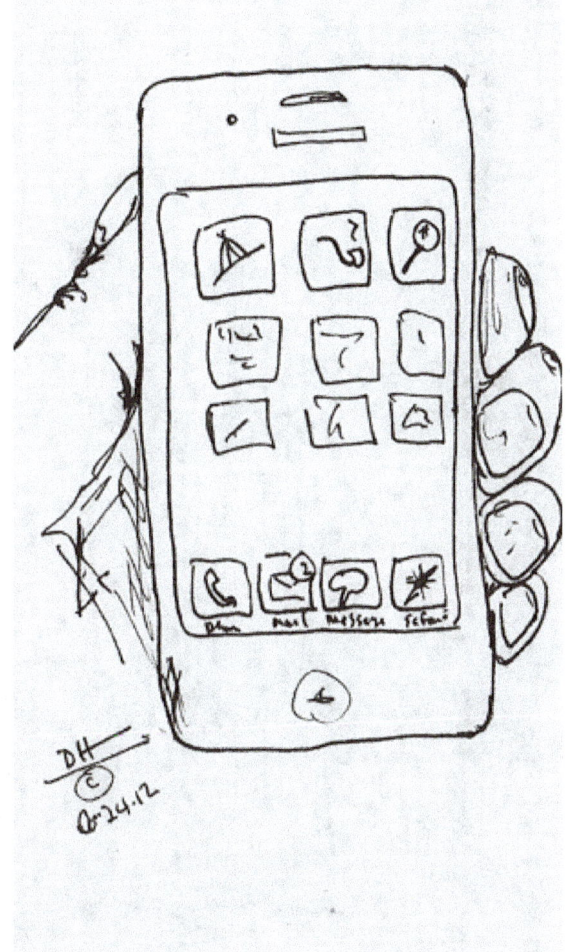

"…Thanks to the telephone and the help of the Yard, I can usually get my essentials without leaving this room…" RETI

Sherlock Holmes
Channelling Popeye

"...The sailor stood looking at him with puckered eyes..." GLOR

Sherlock Holmes Uses
Waterford Crystal

"...It's all clear as crystal, as you put it..." NORW

Sherlock Holmes Loves Sock Monkey

"...It was the monkey not the professor..." CREE

Sherlock Holmes
On Steroids

"...The other, a bull-necked youth with course, bloated
features..." STUD

Sherlock Holmes
Dias de los Muertos

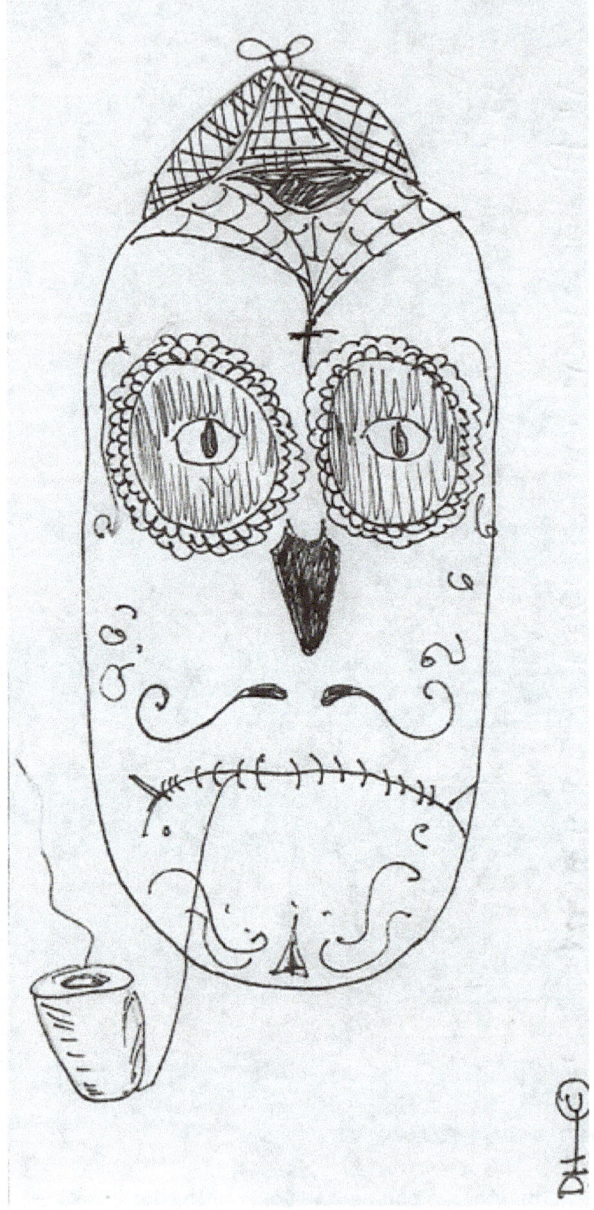

"...He's a man dead – there's no denying it..." GOLD

Sherlock Holmes
Troll Doll

"...The whole incident left a most ugly impression upon
my mind..." GLOR

Sherlock Holmes
Visits Ft. Worth

"...do you remember seeing any cow-tracks today?..."
PRIO

www.ingramcontent.com/pod-product-compliance
Lightning Source LLC
Chambersburg PA
CBHW071329250626
47159CB00004B/1534